AARON CAHOON

The Epiphany Colony

The Murder of Vincent Cortez

Contents

Prologue

A glass bottle smashed against the wall of the tavern, inches away from Brad Asher's head. The kind of thing Brad had gotten used to over the course of his career as a private detective. It did not matter what he was investigating: unfaithful spouses, thefts, or even missing pets. Four cases out of five, Brad would end up following someone, he would eventually get their attention and ask a few questions, and as soon as they figured out what was up, that someone would either turn violent or take off running.

Or in this case, both.

Because, naturally, the bottle was only a distraction. The suspect, under suspicion for the disappearance of twenty pounds of bacon (that is, real pork bacon, a shockingly precious commodity in the colony) during his shift at the local grocer, responded poorly to Brad's questioning.

Then again, who responds well to a person showing up to your favorite dive not-so-subtly accusing you of stealing a luxury item from your place of work? Admittedly the approach was never Brad's strong suit.

"Hey, are you Stephen?" Asher had asked, sliding up to the young blonde man seated at a table in the corner of the bar.

"Yeah, and you're Asher. The colony's not that big, man, I've seen you around."

"Hey, there's a few thousand people here! I sure haven't had the chance to interact with everyone yet!" This wasn't inaccurate. Although Asher had resided at the colony for about a year, most of the people he had interacted with were the aforementioned criminals and cheaters, or their victims. Up until this point, Stephen Tucker had been neither.

"Look, what do you want? Can't you see I'm busy?"

"You sure don't look busy. You're almost to the bottom of that beer. I'm sure you can spare a few minutes to answer some questions."

"I just got off work and I'm trying to relax before I head back to do it all again tomorrow. Or maybe your glamorous life as a private investigator has made you forget about how soul-crushing retail work can be?"

That's a bit unfair, thought Asher. *You get yelled at by customers. I get yelled at by the people I'm investigating. It's at least equal, right?*

"Okay fine, we can skip the small talk, it's about your job. You wouldn't happen to know anything about the missing bacon?"

"Why would I?" Stephen asked, appearing disinterested.

"Seems like it would be a hot piece of gossip. Something that would be all over the breakroom."

"Yeah, well, I don't really gossip or hang out in the breakroom at work. Don't talk much to the people I work with in general, really."

This statement struck Brad as a bit odd. At twenty-one Earth years old, Stephen Tucker was not hard to look at. Then again if he was half as standoffish with his coworkers as he was being towards Brad...

"You haven't even heard people talking about it at work? It's the talk of the town! I mean, how does a twenty pound box of bacon just up and vanish?"

"How does anybody even know about the shipment of bacon when there's only one box?" Stephen fired back defensively, before realizing what he had just said.

"And how do you know there was only one box? Don't bother answering, I already know. You were on freight duty that day. You probably saw the box, visions of cash and a ticket off this rock dancing in your eyes, am I wrong?"

"You're bluffing, there's no way you can prove any of that!"

"Your own work schedule provided by your boss, the one who contracted me, is all the proof anyone needs. There's also the cameras. At the very least you could have waited to steal the bacon until you had a clear escape route. After all, you said it yourself, the colony isn't that big," Asher finished with a grin.

After what seemed like an eternity of staring at one-another, this was when the bottle flew, Stephen making a beeline for the door.

Brad quickly ducked out of the way of the bottle (though not without getting splashed with some of the dregs of the bottle, this was going to be a pain to get out of his suit later) and started to dash after Stephen.

This was Brad's favorite part. If his marks were going to either turn violent or try to flee, Brad would much rather them flee, tiring themselves out in the process. It would be much easier to fight someone who already wore themselves out.

At least, Brad loved this part in theory. In reality, he still sometimes struggled with navigating this damn city, especially in the late evening when everyone was hanging out in the nightlife district. While he certainly planned to let Stephen tucker himself out, if he let Stephen get too far ahead he might lose him in the crowd and winding streets.

Stephen stopped every few seconds to throw something back at Brad leaving Brad with the difficult snap decision of trying to dodge, catch, or even get hit on purpose in order to stop other people from getting hurt. Which was certainly not helping.

If I can just lure him out of the nightlife district...

Brad didn't have time to finish that thought. As he rounded a corner down another alleyway he saw the flash of a steel pipe flying toward him.

Brad quickly dropped to the ground, wincing at the rush of air inches above his head. *He certainly changed his strategy quickly.*

This usually happened when the suspect gave up on running, but in this case it was more likely that Stephen knew he would never be able to outrun Brad for long.

Better stop toying with him...

At this thought, Brad quickly turned over to his side and planted his hand, kicking off the wall of the alley to add speed and power to his sweep. While it didn't have enough momentum to completely topple Stephen, Brad let his instincts dictate his next move as he quickly spun his other leg over his target, looping around his neck.

Where the head goes, the rest will follow.

His old teacher's words freshly echoing in his mind, Brad finished the takedown by jerking the rest of his body to the side, pulling Stephen's head down to the ground.

While Brad wasn't particularly physically strong, being a five foot eleven beanpole, his true strength came from his flexibility and training in a mix of capoeira, Brazilian jiu jitsu, and taekwondo. He would never present an impressive score on a punching machine, but he at least never had to worry in the case of ground control, so long as his target wasn't significantly stronger or as well-trained as him.

"Let's keep this easy," Brad said to his freshly pinned opponent. "Just return the bacon and your boss is willing to let this go without turning you into the authorities. He said he considered the contract with me a favor for you because you're so young and not normally up to trouble."

"Go to hell. I don't have it anymore." Stephen spat back.

"Pardon?"

"I said I don't have it anymore! I tried to sell it and got swindled. Why do you think I'm still on this shitheap of a rock?"

Dammit, that's gonna make things a lot more complicated.

"Well, that's unfortunate. I'm probably going to get my pay docked a bit for this, but that's the nature of the beast I guess."

Brad reached into his pocket for his communicator, but the local police were on the scene before he had a chance to make the call.

"Brad Asher," a familiar female voice came from behind him, "I should have guessed that the lack of discretion was your doing."

"Oh, hi Elaine," Brad said, attempting an air of nonchalance. "I found the bacon thief."

"Is that supposed to make me feel better after you shoved some poor man out of the way in your chase?"

Brad quickly ran through the encounter in his mind again, before sheepishly admitting, "Oh yeah, I guess that did happen. To be honest the whole thing was a blur. I was probably trying to save him from getting his face smashed in with a brick."

"Uh-huh, whatever you say," Elaine muttered. "By the way, I'd prefer it if you referred to me as Officer Seol around civilians."

"Huh, normally you're harping on me to call you seonsaeng-nim."

"That's in class you dolt. Stop being cheeky. Now get off the suspect and let me cuff him so I can take him in. You go let Mr. Valentine know that his bacon thief is in custody. We'll talk later."

"Yeah," Brad said, standing. "Later."

—

Elaine Seol was an old friend of Brad's from his school days. She had gone into training to become a police officer while Brad had struggled with his previous line of work, getting into medical school and becoming a doctor.

Elaine was actually the one who recommended that Brad move

to the Epiphany Colony. She had been assigned there a few years prior as a police officer, advancing to the rank of lieutenant. Initially she wanted Brad to undergo training to become an officer like herself, but Brad declined. Eventually she was able to talk him into setting up shop as a private detective.

The Epiphany Colony was the third in a series of colonies set up in orbit around Mars and her moons called the Chronicles Project. The Epiphany was the first of these, matching orbit with Deimos for the purposes of mining and exploration, and while the colony had been around long enough to have a structured police force as well as fire and rescue within its domed walls, it was also far enough removed from the rest of the Earth-based Federation that jobs were given based less on documented qualification and more on what skills the voluntary colonists had, existing in an awkward half-step between being a full frontier colony and being a fully-recognized state within the dominion of the Federation, lacking the metaphorical Golden Spike that would finally join Earth and Mars in unity.

That more than anything else was what appealed to Brad. Maybe he couldn't make his momma proud by becoming a doctor, but at least he could enjoy the idea of being his own boss, assuming he was able to keep work coming in.

Turns out Elaine had been right all along, as thefts and infidelity seemed to be fairly routine.

* * *

Mr. Ziggy Valentine, the owner of the grocery store, a tall, thin, brown-haired man in his...thirties? Forties? Fifties? Brad was never sure because the man seemed weirdly ageless. Whatever his age, he did not take kindly to the news of Stephen's arrest.

"I'd been hoping that you would have been able to solve this problem without getting the police involved," the tall, elflike Valentine said.

"I was trying to, but then the kid decided to make a scene, and it turns out he'd already lost the bacon by the time I caught up to him."

"It's been less than a week since the theft, how did he manage that?" Valentine asked incredulously.

"He said he got swindled trying to sell it, so someone out there is enjoying a nice breakfast on your store's dime, unfortunately."

"This is inconceivable. I don't know if I'm more upset with you or that dumbass of an employee of mine for getting mixed up with the wrong crowd. But a contract is a contract. The full fee will be wired into your account tomorrow morning. 50,000 credits. Don't spend it all in one place. Unless that place is my store."

"Thank you kindly. The inbox is always open if you need more stuff investigated."

"I'll think about it," Valentine replied unconvincingly.

Chapter 1

"Thought you'd never show up," Elaine muttered as Brad finally walked into her apartment.

"I had to take a shower and change," Brad replied in an annoyed tone. "I didn't want to show up smelling like beer, especially that rancid stuff they sell down at the Steel Ball."

"You shouldn't knock it. It grows on you after a while." Elaine chuckled.

"I hate the taste of beer anyway. Maybe I'll check out their wine selection next time I'm there for pleasure. Whenever that is."

"Once a snob, always a snob," Elaine muttered.

"What? I don't like beer and I always feel awkward in that place. You know about a third of their customer base has tried to kill me, right?" Brad fired back defensively.

"Oh, come on, they have other stuff to drink, it's not that bad. I go in there all the time and people don't hassle me, and I'm pretty sure I've arrested all of those same people."

"Yeah, yeah, the difference being you have an entire squad of police officers who would kindly rearrest every single one of them if something happened to you. I've got no such backup."

"Your choice to not come forward about our friendship here."

"We can! Eventually. It just doesn't feel like the right time yet. I'm still not sure how to go about mixing business with pleasure publicly. At any rate I feel like my clientele might be a bit hesitant to trust someone whose primary informant is a police officer."

"Come on, don't act like you came here just so you could live out of your office as a private investigator. You came for me, and we both know that."

Okay, so the "being one's own boss thing" was only half the reason.

"Speaking of mixing business and pleasure, though, I know we're off the clock and you don't like to talk about work off the clock…"

Here it goes, Brad thought, preparing himself for another chew-out session regarding the man who got injured. *You need to show more restraint. You need to be careful of people getting caught in the crossfire. Blah blah blah.* It was all stuff he had heard before.

"I have a request for you that's off the books."

"Look, I'm sorry—wait what?" Brad blinked. *Well, this isn't what I was expecting.*

"I have an anonymous request for you as Brad Asher the detective. One I definitely can't make as a police lieutenant."

"I...umm...I'm listening."

They sat in silence for a bit while Elaine searched for the words.

Brad shifted uneasily in his seat at Elaine's table. "So what's the request?" he pressed, hoping that that might spur the conversation along.

Elaine leaned forward, sighing. "There's no easy way to put this. There's a murder–"

Brad quickly interrupted, "Nope, I don't do murders, you know that."

"You didn't even hear the full details," Elaine muttered.

"I'm not sure I *need* to hear the full details," Brad replied, frowning. "You know how badly people react when I investigate them for small stuff. I don't even own a gun, how the hell am I supposed to protect myself from a murderer? You're the police officer, why aren't you guys investigating it?"

"We *did*," Elaine responded defensively.

"Excuse me?"

"The department *did* investigate it," she said more firmly.

Brad sat silently for a bit, before finally saying, "Okay, let's start at the beginning."

Elaine leaned back and cleared her throat.

"So, you know the evidence officer, Jill Cortez?"

Brad stopped to think, trying to remember all the different members of the police force he had had the chance to speak with. "Yeah, I think you introduced me to her when I first moved here, but I haven't really dealt with her much otherwise. Why?"

"Well, the *official* story is that she killed her husband, the reporter Vincent Cortez."

Brad recoiled. He had worked with Vincent in the past, as reporters made for great info brokers and rumormongers, but he hadn't put two and two together that Vincent was married to Elaine's colleague Jill. But something had felt out of sorts in the last couple weeks. Recently Brad had noticed that Vincent's columns in the local newscasts were rather quiet, but no official word had gotten out.

"When did this happen?" Brad asked, showing more sincere interest.

"Only in the last couple weeks. I'm not surprised you didn't know, though, because the department is trying to keep a lid on it. That's one of quite a few things that have made me raise an eyebrow." Elaine took a drink from the wine she poured at the beginning of the conversation. "The more I think about it, the less sense it makes."

Brad leaned forward. "Well, what else can you tell me? How did he die? Did they have a poor relationship? Where is Jill now?"

"They've still got Jill in custody. The whole thing is fishy, though. The secrecy, as well as this coming out of the blue. As far as I know, they had a great relationship, but the official cause of death is blood loss from a gunshot wound. The ballistics profile matches her personal .45. And the weapon itself was confiscated and examined, and while it was obviously covered in her fingerprints, no other prints were found on the weapon."

Brad frowned. "Seems like a pretty open and shut case. Why's the department being so secretive about it, then?"

"That's what bugs me! They shouldn't need to!" What composure Elaine had had up to this point melted away to a combination of frustration and grief.

"Okay, you might have convinced me. Have you talked to Jill at all since she was detained?"

"Only a little, but she won't give me a straight answer to any of my questions." Elaine sighed. "She seems like she's all but given up, though who could blame her?"

"Sounds like she could use a lawyer more than a private investigator," Brad muttered thoughtfully.

Elaine rolled her eyes. "Brilliant deduction, Sherlock. If only I was wise enough to have considered that myself! Do you have a recommendation? Because I sure as hell don't."

Brad reeled back at the sarcastic outburst. "Okay, okay, I'm sorry, I didn't mean it like that. I mean I'm not sure what I can add to the investigation."

"Just a quick run-through to find anything we missed. Maybe since you're not affiliated with the police force, Cortez will actually answer your questions." Elaine sank into her seat.

After a bit, Brad finally said, "Okay, I'll at least see if I can ask her a few questions. Still, this is an off the books, possibly dangerous investigation. And since you're already breaking my policy about talking about work outside of work...let's talk about payment."

"Don't worry, I can swing it. Baseline 50,000 plus an added premium of 100,000 for danger involved. I understand you have to keep the lights on and pay for your own healthcare in the event that something goes wrong. Naturally, payment on completion of the task as usual. I really had to dip into my savings for this so don't half-ass the investigation, or I'll know."

"Do I ever?" Brad asked.

"Do you really want me to answer that?" Elaine fired back, playfully.

Brad paused, before finally saying, "Fair enough. Well, it's getting late and even though this investigation is off the books, I still have a bunch of stuff to organize to begin the case, so I think I'm going to head back to my place. Will you be able to let me into the detention center tomorrow to speak with Cortez?"

"I'll see what I can do."

* * *

The office of Brad Asher, Private Investigator, in a stark contrast to Elaine's neat, recently-built apartment building, was in a dingy, older part of the colony, being one of the few places Brad could get a decent lease with what little money he had upon moving to the colony. The interior wasn't much, just three rooms: the main lobby/office area, a modest bathroom with a shower compartment, and a smaller private office which Brad mainly used as his personal quarters. There wasn't much to it: a futon for sleeping, a viewscreen for whatever news or entertainment broadcasts he would peruse, a small wardrobe with what little clothing he brought with him to the colony, and a mirror. That he barely used. That one was a gift. The gift that kept on giving, as he was constantly reminded of how disheveled and tired he looked.

Because he mainly used the "private office" for sleeping, he spent most of his time in the main room, where he had a cheap desk that he had to assemble himself when he purchased it, a computer that worked just well enough that he could get his work done without having to bang on it too much, and a couple couches in the sitting area that were, in all honesty, significantly more comfortable than his own futon. To the point that he often slept on them when he was feeling particularly lazy or had had too much to drink. From the ceiling hung another viewscreen in the vain hope that he could entertain any extra clients waiting for his attention. Should that day he had extra clients waiting for his attention ever arise. But since most requests came through email anyway, this was more or less a wasted feature. Maybe he could use it to host friends when the big game was on.

Should the day he had friends to host who all had the same sports interests ever arise.

Upon arrival into the office, Brad began his evening ritual. Lock the door. Boot up the computer to check for messages. No messages. Put some music on the speakers throughout the office. A little jazz. Take a shower. An extra few minutes. He'd earned it. Check the news. Nothing noteworthy besides an interview with Valentine about Bacon Boy. Poor kid was probably going to be spending quite a while behind bars for that slipup. Shame.

And yet, slow news day as it was, there was absolutely no coverage of Vincent Cortez. Surely someone would at least put up a memorial broadcast. Right? Instead it seemed like every news source on the colony (and several off-colony) were trying their best to pretend the man never existed to begin with.

I guess that settles it. Hopefully I don't make too much of a nuisance of myself at the police station.

Chapter 2

Brad awoke to the alarm he had set the night before. Accounting for a desire to get a full eight hours' sleep and the fact that he finally got to bed at about 12:30, he set the alarm for 9:00 AM. Not that the time made much of a difference in terms of natural light, which followed its own schedule.

Instead, to compensate, the colony had its own "faux sun", a series of bright lights at the ceiling of the dome that mimicked the light of the sun as seen on Earth during different parts of the day. So from the perspective of an average citizen, 9 AM on the colony was similar to 9 AM on earth in terms of light.

Brad quickly dressed and sent a message to Elaine asking when the best time to visit the detention center would be before heading out. His stomach growled. Breakfast time.

Man, I wish I got a place with a kitchen.

This line of thinking was more or less part of Brad's morning routine. While he was okay with giving a little money to Elaine to compensate for her cooking so many of his meals, the lack of independence really got to him.

That and food from diners and convenience stores was really expensive for what you were getting. That said, given the case he had just accepted, Brad felt fine indulging just a little bit.

Brad ducked into a local favorite of his, a small diner called Jimbo's, named for the owner, James Bourne, a name made even more hilarious by the Jimbo's own love for spy films from the twentieth and twenty-first centuries.

Jimbo's themed itself after Earth's diners from the 1950's and 1960's. The type that looked like repurposed train cars that were known for the basic American breakfast of pancakes, eggs, bacon, and coffee. In this case, substitute the proteins for a similar synthetic variation that was cheaper and more easily acquired, and while they were advertised as being indistinguishable from the real thing in terms of taste and texture, that was an obvious lie. Someone who had had both would know for sure that something was...off, even if they couldn't place what it was.

But whatever, food is food.

So Brad had the usual. "Bacon", three "eggs", a short stack of pancakes, hash browns (which of course were rehydrated), and a cup of coffee, which was somehow actually real coffee rather than some abomination made from ground mushrooms or dirt or whatever passed as "coffee" in these parts.

That Brad unfortunately would "ruin" in the eyes of Jimbo

himself by adding too much milk (well...”milk”) and sweetener, but Brad wasn't drinking it for the taste, which he actually couldn't stand, but he thought for sure he was going to need the caffeine boost.

While Brad was eating his breakfast, the response from Elaine came to his communicator.

Come anytime between 1000 and 1200.

Small window. Does she really need to write everything in military time? Brad checked the time. 9:35 AM. He could probably make it to the detention center by 10:00 if he left as soon as he finished his breakfast and there was no interruption on the mag rail ride he would have to take. He probably wouldn't be able to get more than a half-hour or so to talk to Cortez, but the more time possible, the better.

—-

Elaine knew what she was doing was going to cause some huge problems for her later on, but considering the lengths the department was going to bury Cortez's arrest, she had to keep reminding herself that it was worth the risk.

Once she arrived at the police station at 0900 she knew she had precious little time to set up a meeting between Asher and Cortez. She quickly set to work “reevaluating” the schedule of duties of those working under her supervision.

I'll just put myself over the detention area for today. Probably looks bad for me to take the job everyone else considers so cushy, but this is one of those few times when I need something done perfectly exactly how I want it done.

Even with this little internal monologue, Elaine knew she was lying to herself. If there was one common criticism that her family, colleagues, and friends could offer about her, it was the fact that she was kind of anal. Whatever. If others had a problem with her always being right, that was their business.

The schedule for the day was outlined. Good. Easy part was finished. At this point, the message she was expecting from Asher came, right on cue.

When would be the best time to swing by?

Elaine pondered this for a second. Time to get to work on the hard part.

Surprisingly, the request to have a stranger meet with Cortez wasn't met with enthusiasm from the current shift lead at the detention center, a younger man named Charlie Ray.

"You of all people know how sensitive this case is, Seol. We can't have too many people in and out of here." Elaine could tell the young man had recited the line many times in front of the mirror, expecting that someone was going to want to see Cortez or another high-profile "guest" in the detention center. She could remember having a similar anxiety when she first started. Elaine almost felt sorry for the kid, especially with what she was about to pull.

"Relax, Ray, I'm the superior officer here. If anything goes wrong, it's my ass." Elaine winked.

Ray stammered, "O...okay, sure. Visiting hours are 1000 to 1200, so if he's able to make it in so quickly, that's when he can. It's your funeral, I guess."

At least he's kind of cute when he tries to play off his insecurity.

"Thanks Ray. You have no idea how helpful this is going to be."

At least that part was true...

— -

As Brad waited to arrive at the police station, a thought suddenly occurred to him. He quickly reached into his jacket pocket for his communication device and fired off a quick message to Elaine.

Does Cortez have any tells?

It wasn't long before his communicator buzzed with another message.

Tells?

Brad glowered. Wasn't Elaine friends with this woman?

C'mon, like in Poker? Tell me you've played cards with the girl!

Some time passed, and then...

I dunno. I guess she doesn't make eye contact well when she's nervous.

Brad's eyes narrowed. An evidence officer that had trouble making eye contact when she was nervous was not what he expected to deal with today.

How did she become a police officer if she doesn't make eye contact when she's nervous?!

Some more time passed, and then...

Does it matter? I've never been able to get her to join us for card night. This is the best I've got!

Brad sighed. It wasn't much better than nothing, but it would have to do.

Elaine was waiting for Brad near the booth he would be using to speak with Cortez. It wasn't long after Brad arrived that Officer Cortez was led to her side of the plexiglass separator. Per someone's request, an old-fashioned American country song from God only knew what decade or century seeped in through some speakers set in the ceiling.

Jill Cortez née Khalil, age 24, had the timid appearance and attitude of one who definitely shouldn't be behind bars. Probably one who shouldn't be working for the police, either, but obviously it was too late to turn that around. Besides her silky, straight hair, everything about her was the picture of "mouse", from her small frame to the thick spectacles she wore. Brad wasn't sure she was capable of hurting a fly, let alone the supposed love of her life.

Either she's completely innocent or she's a really good method actor.

"Hey Cortez," Elaine began. "I just wanted to ask you a few more questions."

"Is he a cop?" Jill asked, pensively, clearly not wanting to be here.

"Have you *seen* him around the precinct?"

"No, but...well," she looked away.

Elaine chuckled awkwardly, trying to restore some form of amiable atmosphere. "Relax, Cortez, you've met him before, the one time. That friend of mine that moved here about a year ago."

Brad nodded. "Brad Asher. Relax, I'm a private investigator. I'm not affiliated with the police, and most of them don't seem to like me that much as it is.

"Why are you here, then? The case against me is pretty airtight, isn't it?" Her tone of voice communicated clearly a feeling of defeat. She wasn't even looking at Brad when she said it.

"Yeah, Elaine filled me in, but there were a few things that kind of left me confused so I wanted some clarity. I guess I'll start with the obvious." Brad leaned forward, almost to emphasize his question. "Did you do it?"

Elaine fired a shocked look in Brad's direction. Cortez, conversely, just looked confused.

"What do you mean?" Cortez asked, almost in disbelief.

"Exactly what I said," Brad said flatly. "Did. You. Do. It? I can't really do much for you if you're actually guilty."

"You say that like you're a lawyer."

Brad leaned back a bit in surprise at the statement. "Honestly I think you'd want a lawyer more if you did it, personally, but I guess I get what you mean. Either way, it's a time and energy thing. I don't want to put forth a bunch of time and resources into a case I can't solve. However, Elaine says you didn't do it, and I've always thought she was a good judge of character. That's why I'm here."

Elaine glowered a bit before nodding. "It's true. I don't buy the 'official story' at all."

Tears welled up in Jill's eyes, as she squeaked, "Would you believe me if I said I didn't do it?"

Brad let the question hang in the air before finally saying, "Okay, this is something I can work with."

Chapter 3

Brad continued, "So, you didn't do it. Can you tell me what happened from your perspective?"

Cortez wiped the tears from her eyes. "I dunno, it's all a bit of a blur. Things just happened so fast that I wasn't able to really process them properly."

Brad looked at Elaine, who nodded, and then he said, "It's okay, just tell us what you can remember. Take your time."

"Well...I was home late from work that day. Something in the evidence locker got misplaced and I had to find it and put it back. I decided I'd surprise Vince with dinner from his favorite restaurant, so I took a little longer getting home than normal. When I made it to the apartment, the place was a mess. The official story is that Vince and I had an argument that got physical before I shot him in self-defense. You ever seen the musical *Chicago*, with the song "We Both Reached For The Gun"? Kind of one of those situations. That's...what they say anyway..." Cortez trailed off.

Brad opened his mouth to point out that the story she was referencing was a fabrication for the sake of convenience, but stopped himself. That was probably the point.

Elaine leaned forward. "But...?"

"That's just it, though. Vince and I never fight. Never fought... that is. Sure, we had disagreements now and then, like all couples do, but it was never...never like that. He would never raise a hand against me, nor I him. That's just...not how we handled things."

Brad looked Cortez over, noting that something was missing. "The report says that the fight got physical, but...you look fine. No bruises or anything. How do they explain that?"

Cortez sat up straight, "Oh yes, let me continue. When I got home, the apartment was...a mess, like I said. In the kitchen I found Vince...he...he was already gone. Shot in the throat. Thank God it was probably over quickly, but..." she sniffled, her voice breaking. "By him was a chef's knife...the one he'd bought for my birthday. Real steel, not ceramic. He knew I was trying to learn more recipes..."

Elaine finished for Cortez, "So the official story is that he grabbed the knife when things got too heated and trashed the place chasing you around, but you put him down before he could get you first." It wasn't a question, as she had read the report previously.

Cortez nodded. "This was when the police showed up in

response to noise complaints as well as the sound from the gunshot. Before I knew it, I was in cuffs in the back of a cruiser. No matter what I said, they wouldn't listen. After all, the murder weapon was my own gun, covered in my prints..." Cortez sank into her chair, laying her chin on the table.

"And unable to be fired by anyone but you because of the ID tagging system," Elaine finished, mainly for Brad's benefit.

Brad raised an eyebrow.

"Police firearms have fail-safes installed on them for the safety of the officer. Basically, each piece is registered to one specific officer's individual fingerprints and other biometric data. That way, they can't be fired by someone else, such as, say, a suspect in a scuffle with an officer. If someone who isn't the registered owner of the piece tries to use it, the safety can't be deactivated."

Brad nodded, "I guess that makes sense. Only..." he stroked his chin. "How could it have been your piece if you had just gotten off duty. Wouldn't it be on your person when all this went down?"

Cortez looked down at the floor. "That's what I don't get. They say the ballistics profile is a perfect match. And conveniently," she chuckled, barely masking the pain, "Nobody actually saw how it happened, so this was all pieced together by the officers on scene."

"That *is* convenient," said Brad, before clarifying at the death-glare coming from Elaine, "Nobody saw it happen, but all evidence points to you. It is your word against the law, and the only cases of reasonable doubt come from people who know you. Which is always said about convicts by their friends and families. That they'd never do such a thing, I mean. Seems like they have you dead-to-rights. I see two possibilities."

Cortez and Elaine both blinked.

"Either you're guilty as sin. Or this is the perfect crime. Do you know anyone who would want to hurt you or Vince?"

Cortez looked at the ceiling, trying to gather her thoughts. "I mean...Vince was a journalist who a lot of people accused of being 'too nosy for his own good', and I work for the police department which always has people upset at it. So there are plenty of reasons for people to not like us. But I can't think of anyone who would want either of us *dead*."

Elaine straightened up suddenly. "Is there anything that Vince was investigating that people would have not wanted him to see?"

Cortez furrowed her brow. "I mean...maybe? He didn't tell me everything about his work." She sighed. " Some things, sure, once things were out in the open, but he was really secretive about a lot of his work. Maybe he was just protecting me."

Brad rubbed his chin, thoughtfully. "Any chance you have access to his work files?"

Cortez narrowed her eyes and waved her hands, almost to say,

"Jail, duh." If Brad could slap himself without looking crazy, he would have.

"I mean...did he keep his files in the house, or is there anything in his office?" Brad clarified frantically, trying to keep his professional demeanor. "Did he keep backups, or notes, or anything like that? Anything will help."

Elaine shook her head. "I'm not sure, but I'd recommend you search our apartment. Well, for anything that's still left following the break-in and investigation. The door code is 2215."

"2215?"

"Yes. It's the year we got married. We have to make sure we remember our anniversary, right...?" She broke into tears again.

Brad looked Cortez in the eyes, those pretty brown eyes, and said, "I know it's too much to ask you not to worry, but we're going to get you out of here, and we're going to bring your husband's killers to justice."

Elaine smiled, "Yeah, they'll rue the day they decided to mess with your family!" she exclaimed, trying to inject some pep and positivity into the conversation.

"Th...thank you, both of you," Jill squeaked.

—-

After Cortez was taken back to her cell, Brad turned to Elaine and said, "I'm going to head straight to her apartment. Hopefully I can find something worth our time. Or at least, somewhat interesting or helpful."

"Don't you want to wait for me to get off work so we can go together?" Elaine asked, mildly disappointed.

"There's not enough time, and I think it would be better if you were here to keep an eye on Jill. If Vince truly was investigating something someone didn't want him to know about, Jill might be next." Brad's intense expression caught Elaine somewhat off guard. She still wasn't used to "detective Brad" and his way of doing things.

Elaine paused, and then said, "Okay, but be careful. I've tried to keep this meeting as low-profile as I could, but..." she trailed off before finishing, "Just watch your back, okay? And call me *immediately* if something even remotely fishy happens."

Chapter 4

Jill and Vincent's apartment was a few blocks away from Brad's office, something Brad found to be kind of odd. Sure, Vincent Cortez was an independent journalist who had some columns in various newspapers, likely not a super lucrative position, but the money Jill would make as an evidence officer should more than make up for it, right?

As Brad considered just why someone would willingly live in this neighborhood when they could likely afford better housing, he noticed his reflection in the window of a shop, or to be more specific, he noticed the reflection of a man wearing a baseball cap with the brim low, trying to block his face.

There's the look of someone who's up to no good.

Brad, not sure of how long the other man had been following him, quickly began considering his options.

I could make a scene. There are enough people around that he wouldn't dare doing something if I got their attention.

Then again...if I scare him off I won't be able to question him.

Brad quickly looked over his shoulder at the man, who looked at the screen of his communicator, trying to "act naturally". The man was about six-feet-six-inches, wearing a loose hooded sweater, hiding his physique. Possibly hiding a weapon as well.

A gun wouldn't be as likely. Anything manufactured in the colony itself would be so heavily monitored that an investigation would only really be a formality, and the cost of importing things from off-colony was prohibitively expensive, not likely to be within the means of your common street thug. This is to say nothing about the cost of ammunition in addition to the cost of the firearm itself. And while laser weapons were in an experimental phase, they too were extremely rare, expensive, and unreliable to be worth the effort of obtaining for anyone besides the staunchest of enthusiasts. Brad doubted this guy had the money to be in that club.

There was the possibility for weapons to have been smuggled onto the colony. But a smuggling ring like that would probably require an inside man in the police force or the military.

Now there's an idea...

Brad quickly ran over the scenario in his head.

If I don't head straight to the apartment he'll know I'm onto him for sure and may try to peel off at the first sign I'm deviating from his script. On the other hand I don't know if there's someone else waiting for me at the apartment.

Brad covertly looked the man over through the reflection in a nearby window. He had Brad beat in size, for sure.

If I get the jump on him it might not be too bad, but in a "fair" fight things could get much uglier.

Standing at five-foot-ten, Brad wasn't small by any stretch, but his skinny, lanky frame would have made him about as effective in a fair one-on-one brawl as a loose coat, ironically with half the durability. No, this would require some cheating from Brad.

Well, nothing ventured.

Brad took out his communication device and quickly sent a message to Elaine.

Got company. Going to Jill's place anyway. Send help if you don't hear from me in the next hour.

An hour was probably too much time. Assuming nothing went wrong, he would probably be in and out in twenty, thirty minutes tops, and if Mr. Ballcap proved to be as much of a nuisance as Brad anticipated, an hour would make no more difference than five to ten minutes for Brad's freshly caved-in skull. Brad shuddered at the thought. No, he definitely had a plan. Get in, get out, and if he were to get attacked, get out faster.

Brad eventually made his way to the apartment in question. The building itself wasn't terribly large, only three stories, annoyingly with Cortez's apartment on the top floor. No elevator. Of course. Moving into this place was probably a pain. Brad sighed and made his way to the third floor, finding himself in front of the entrance to Cortez's apartment. Sure enough, the code given by Cortez opened the door immediately, so Brad let himself in.

Although he had expected the apartment to be a dump characteristic of this part of the colony, the truth is it wasn't terrible. Two bedrooms. Fairly large sitting area. Freshly redone walls, floors, and doors, at least compared to Brad's office which had seen no repairs, upgrades, or remodels since he had moved in. Even the furniture looked to have been purchased in the last few years. It was spacious. Clearly meant for the family Cortez was hoping to have soon. Though to be fair anything was "spacious" compared to the shoeboxes that most people in this older part of the colony lived in, usually repurposed from the spartan barracks of the colony's infancy.

The place would have been quite nice if it hadn't been completely torn to pieces. Belongings strewn about, blood all over the carpet. The body had been removed, but thankfully the body wasn't what Brad was there for.

I'm kind of amazed the cleanup crew hasn't been here yet though...

Brad found a computer terminal in the spare bedroom, which had been fashioned into a makeshift office. Not a bad place to get work done from home, though it could be troublesome once a baby was on the way. The room itself had all the makings of an independent journalist's office. Books strewn about. Conspiracy board on the wall linking different people to different things. Brad took a closer look at it but nothing really stuck out amidst the red string and photos. He would need Vince around to interpret just what the hell he was looking at, assuming it was at all relevant to his investigation in the first place. That ship was freshly sunk.

Let's try the computer.

The computer booted up quickly, but of course the first thing that popped onto the screen was a password field.

Crap. Forgot to ask if Jill knew her hubby's password.

Brad fired off a message to Elaine asking her to ask for the password and continued trying to break into the computer. He quickly typed in a few things off the top of his head. Various combinations of the couple's names, their anniversary date, nothing was working.

Of course he made his password impossible to brute force. Guess I'm gonna need to call in a favor on this. Fan–freaking–tastic.

He powered the terminal down, opened it up with the toolkit he made sure to have in his jacket, and unseated the hard drive, which thankfully wasn't too packed in compared to some other computers Brad had had the displeasure of popping open, his own included whenever it went on the fritz.

Breaking and entering, as well as theft. I'm really on a roll today. This is gonna look mighty fishy if Elaine can't keep the cleaners off my back.

As Brad slipped the hard drive into his jacket pocket, he took a look at the time. He had arrived at the apartment at about 1 PM, and he had sat at the computer trying to brute force the password for about twenty minutes.

So far, so good. Maybe I won't need the backup I asked for after all. Though I'm kind of surprised my paparazzo didn't take the bait. He's gotta be waiting for me somewhere.

Brad shot off another message to Elaine.

I couldn't figure out the password to access the computer so I'm stealing the hard drive. I may know someone who can help me retrieve whatever is on it, though I'm not looking forward to that headache. We'll burn that bridge when we get to it.

Sliding the communicator back into his pocket, Brad started towards the entrance of the apartment. He had scarcely opened the door and stepped out onto the apartment building's landing before catching the glint of steel in the corner of his eye.

Instinctively he faded backwards, barely avoiding the telescopic baton swung by the man he had seen earlier.

Ah, there he is, right on time.

Brad quickly looked over his surroundings. Nothing to grab to use as a weapon. Being on the third floor, jumping over the railing could be a bit dicey. It looked to be about a twenty foot drop.

The man swung at him again with the baton, smashing part of the doorway. Brad stole an opportunity to deliver a kick to the man's side, his leg harmlessly bouncing off the man's surprisingly thick physique. He was definitely wearing something heavy under that hoodie, whether it was a thick shirt or a bulletproof vest.

The man seized a chance while Brad reeled, swinging the baton again. Brad tucked and rolled to the side, trying to deliver a quick sweeping kick to the man's ankles. The man quickly stepped out of the way. Brad cursed, scanning his surroundings for something to turn the tide, quickly dodging another swing from the baton.

In the corner of his eye, Brad noticed a large, thirteen-by-twenty inch photograph of the happy couple in an expensive-looking frame. Gaudy, sure, but Brad could make use of it. He grabbed it off the wall and smashed it into his assailant's face.

Mr. Ballcap screamed out in pain as glass and wood cut into his face.

Time for a cheap shot...

Brad quickly spun around, launching the heel of his right foot directly into the man's groin. As the man doubled over screaming in pain, Brad quickly smashed him again with the photo frame, knocking him to the ground, where he lay still.

Brad silently cursed, wishing he had thought to bring something to tie the man up with, a set of handcuffs, a rope, something, but considering Brad hadn't expected to get in a fight today, he would have to find a chance later. Brad quickly sprinted towards the stairway and made his way down to the ground floor, more jumping down the stairs than running down them.

Brad quickly pulled his communicator out, meaning to update Elaine on what happened to him, but during the struggle Brad must have missed his notification ring, because there was a message from Elaine.

Jill's dead. Someone shot her.

Brad cursed again. This day just kept getting better and better...

Chapter 5

After sending the message, Elaine put out a general alert message to all officers that Cortez had been shot and that the killer was at large, likely still within the detention center. Alarms began blaring. Red warning lights began shining throughout the facility. Though she couldn't hear it, Elaine also knew that, per department policy, all exits would be locked.

She knew she couldn't 100% rely on this plan working. If, God forbid, the culprit was inside the department from the beginning as she had been suspecting, they would already have planned around the standard operating procedure in emergency situations to make their escape before the alarm was raised. They would know the playbook, step-by-step and would already be at least one step ahead. But if there was any chance of stopping them from getting out, Elaine knew she had to take that chance.

While she had her communicator out, Elaine pulled up the security cameras for the facility. One perk of her rank was remote access to the automated security systems in government facilities. As she quickly flipped through the different cameras assigned to the detention center, her mind quickly raced trying to figure out what sort of timing the murder would have happened in. When checking to see if she still had a pulse, Elaine noted that Cortez was still warm, so it couldn't have been long. Just long enough that she had passed due to blood-loss or brain injury. Either way, she wasn't coming back.

Fortunately the facility itself wasn't particularly large, nor was it meant to hold prisoners long-term. If a crime went to trial and the accused were found guilty, their long-term sentencing would typically be implemented off-colony, typically in orbital prison stations throughout the solar system, if they were lucky. Some prisoners would end up on colony planets conducting hard labor, a practice Elaine couldn't stand. As if humanity had failed to learn from the previous centuries of that inane practice.

Assuming the crime wasn't bad enough for execution, anyway, though capital punishment was a very rare conviction following decades of debate before the colonies were even launched. In a legal, official sense, the death penalty was reserved for the most egregious crimes. Which isn't to say that that was all people would die for during the age of colonies. Specifically, a lot of what was affectionately called frontier justice occurred off-the-books in the early days of the colonies, mainly because of the length of time proper extradition of prisoners would take. This off-the-books prairie justice also tended to dip into the realm of cruel and unusual punishment, "befitting the crime" as was often joked by those who partook in the practice.

Elaine paused to think about this. If the killer was part of the force, was it motivated by some desire for frontier justice? No, it couldn't have been. As far as Elaine knew, Vince wasn't a criminal, and Jill sure as hell wasn't either. The girl was barely cut out to be a police officer. No way she could be wrapped up in some crime ring.. Just what had Vincent Cortez discovered?

Elaine looked solemnly at Jill Cortez's body. The poor girl didn't know anything. Or if she did, she never let on. She was just collateral damage.

Don't worry, I'm not gonna let this slide.

Elaine's communicator buzzed. A message from Brad. Finally. She had notified Brad of Cortez's death...fifteen minutes ago?

Huh, I guess it feels like it's been longer.

Elaine looked at Brad's response.

What? Are you safe? I just got jumped.

Elaine slapped her forehead and cursed. She decided to call Brad. Things needed hashed out *now*.

Brad picked up immediately.

"Elaine! God, what happened?"

"Someone shot Cortez, we don't know who it is or where they went." Elaine looked at Brad. "But wait, didn't you say you got jumped? You look fine! Hair's a little messed up, but..."

"Oh, he missed with the baton. He's probably not far behind though. I kicked him in the nuts and bolted. Might be unconscious, but I didn't wanna chance it. Can I call you back when I get to safety?"

"Uh...yeah sure, but hurry up though. I'm locked in the detention center and I think the killer is still with us." Elaine's mind raced. With each passing second, the danger grew.

Brad's eyes widened. "What?! Oh no...look, do what you can to be safe. I'll get back to you when—" Brad suddenly started shouting. "BEHIND YOU!"

Elaine hadn't heard the door open behind her, but she quickly turned to see a woman pointing a gun directly at her. No time to think, Elaine quickly dove to the side as the gun went off, a bullet burrowing into the floor where she had been sitting. Elaine's heart rate shot up, trying to find something she could hide behind. Which, of course, since it was just the holding cell, there wasn't anything. Elaine frantically reached for her stun gun. She only had one shot and not nearly enough time to aim it properly.

Elaine quickly fired off a shot in the shooter's general direction, as white-hot pain shot through her arm up to her shoulder as her arm popped out of its socket in her shoulder.

While in the past, standard issue stun guns were of the taser variety, firing darts attached to wires into the target, incapacitating them via an intense, though usually survivable electric shock, and while those were still commonly in use on the colony due to being relatively inexpensive and easy to manufacture, Elaine had enrolled in a trial for an experimental stun gun that would fire a concussive blast of air at a force similar to that of a shotgun blast, just without the shot spread.

It hurt like hell and recoil was a problem that was well-documented from the trials, as a shotgun blast without a stock to absorb some of the shock would be, but assuming the pressure tank inside the gun didn't fail, it would be much easier to outfit a squad with rather than the disposable cartridges native to tasers.

The upside of the blast was the fact that precision wasn't completely mandatory like it was with a taser. Rather than the taser's very rigid, personalized targeting, the concussive shotgun's blast was very much "Addressed To Whom It May Concern."

The downside being, of course, that firing it from the hip without properly bracing for the blast was an awful, *awful* idea.

While the woman tried to recover from being blasted back into the wall, Elaine quickly dove on top of her and tried to cuff her with her one still-intact arm. Surprisingly, trying to wrestle someone with a dislocated shoulder, even someone as dazed as this woman was, turned out to be surprisingly difficult. This woman might not be all there, but she knew how to handle herself in an up-close scuffle.

Another blast at this range would be a terrible idea. Elaine would never be able to properly brace herself, and the recharge for the air compression tank would take sixty seconds—an eternity in a fight.

Then again, there was one other option.

Elaine reached onto her utility belt for her other non-lethal equipment. Specifically, a bottle of pepper spray. She closed her eyes, held her breath, turned her face away from the spray, and blasted the right in the face.

The woman screamed in agony, letting Elaine know that she now had precious few seconds to finish cuffing the woman. Wrestling her to the ground, Elaine finally managed to pin her in place long enough to cuff her hands behind her back, and then promptly rolled away from what was turning into a very loud, uncoordinated rodeo. Instead, Elaine waited off to the side for a few seconds. Either the woman would pass out from the pain or the spray would wear off. The chemical reaction of the spray would wear off significantly faster than similar sprays used in the past, but it was still difficult to watch this woman writhing in pain. Elaine knew the burning feeling too well from her own training as well as a mishap with the spray on a previous mission.

Eventually the screaming stopped as the woman lost consciousness, and Elaine was finally able to get a good look at her. Another officer, someone she had met recently but couldn't place where from, so Elaine looked her badge up in the department's roster. The woman was a redhead named Jolene Morris. A newer officer, fresh out of the academy. Elaine tried to seek more information but encountered an error.

Server Maintenance—Please Try Again Later

Elaine cursed, slamming her fist into the wall, pain shooting up her arm again. *Okay, yeah that was a bad idea.*

Elaine quickly removed any weaponry from Morris. Pretty brazen of her to barge in here and try to attack Elaine like that. Her aim wasn't particularly great, but she was out for blood for some reason. Surely she didn't think Elaine was the one who killed Cortez, right?

Elaine tried logging into her communicator again. Same orange screen, same error.

Oh for f—wait a minute.

She looked at Morris again. It was a stretch, but she figured she might as well try it. She pulled out Morris' communicator. Nope. Still down. So either both of them were being locked out intentionally, or it was just a legitimate server outage. Either way, timing was *impeccable.*

As she ruminated on this, a squad of officers spilled into the room, arms at the ready. "We heard the commotion. What happened?" the one in front, Ray, asked.

"Morris shot at me. I don't know if she thought I was someone else or what, but I took the liberty of incapacitating her for the time being. We're gonna need to question her when she wakes up so someone make sure she's properly restrained for when the time comes. Meantime, does anyone have anything I can do about this?" She indicated her disabled shoulder. "Or does someone wanna help me get to the infirmary? I think I'm gonna pass out soon and I don't know if I'm gonna make it all the way there myself."

A couple of officers rushed to her side, helping her down the hall to the infirmary. As they walked, Elaine asked, "By the way, is anyone's communicator working? Mine seems to be on the fritz for some reason."

One of the officers in the squad checked his communicator. He shook his head. "No, I'm not getting anything."

"Damn. Were you able to find the one who shot Cortez? Any data on the cameras?"

"No, the cameras went out not long before you notified us about Cortez," the officer replied apologetically.

"Why wasn't I informed?" Elaine fired back incredulously.

"We discovered the outage after you told us to search for the perpetrator. It happened while we were conducting our regular patrol."

Elaine cursed again. "It really is someone who knows our playbook. Although they slipped up. I want everyone in the conference room ASAP." Elaine's mind was already racing. Possibly dulled by the pain so much but Elaine forced herself to stay awake. Call it dedication, call it spite, she wasn't going down until she had this cleared up.

"If it's someone with the kind of clearance to knock out the building's network and cameras, don't you think they'd have gotten out in the confusion?" the officer asked.

"I'm counting on that," Elaine replied. "If one person is missing, we'll know who it is."

Chapter 6

So maybe having someone attempt to reset her shoulder while calling an emergency meeting was a bad idea. It hadn't taken long for everyone currently on-shift to arrive in the conference room, but it was long enough that she was able to have the medic Sanders reset her shoulder and provide her with a sling and a cold pack. She was recommended rest and a warm towel later to relieve the pain, but Elaine put emphasis on the "later" portion of that recommendation. Something needed hashed out, and it needed to be done now.

As people filed into the room she glanced at the roster of officers on duty, carefully marking off each member of the squad as they filed in. Ray, herself, a handful of others, one-by-one were checked off. Morris included that was *almost* everyone. She waited for a bit longer. If this last guy—Marko—walked in, the most likely suspect would be Morris.

A low buzz of conversation settled in over the conference room. Ray and Stephens in particular stood out, being closest to where Elaine was sitting, as they discussed their shock at Officer Morris' actions.

"I dunno man, have you ever really talked to her?" Ray asked. "I mean, she definitely seems nice, but I don't really know much *about* her." Ray folded his arms, frowning.

Stephens shrugged. "She *did* just get transferred in not too long ago. I don't know, nothing about her really strikes me as the type to just up and attack one of her superiors like that, y'know? I feel like there'd be some symptom of that that would come up earlier. Maybe. I dunno, I just want to give her the benefit of the doubt, you get me?"

Elaine watched the door intently. She couldn't decide if she wanted Marko to walk in or not. If he did, that would most likely settle it. Jolene Morris was the killer.

And yet, something about that felt *wrong*. She was brand new, straight out of the academy. She wasn't here long enough to have some sort of grudge against Vince and Jill Cortez. On top of that, although Elaine hadn't worked with her much, if at all, it sounded like those who had would be difficult to convince that she had any sort of penchant for random violence against her colleagues, or that she was some sort of master assassin.

On the other hand, Officer Marko wasn't a particularly good fit for the role of "master hitman" either. He wasn't bad at his job. More...aggressively mediocre.

Elaine tried to access the personnel files again. Still "under maintenance" as the warning was so kind to remind her. Elaine cursed under her breath, ignoring the fact that she suddenly became the center of attention by virtue of her broken silence.

Whoever did this sure wasn't making things any easier.

She was about to prematurely end the meeting to see if she could question Morris when Leonard Marko, a portly, middle-aged officer finally sauntered into the room.

"And just where the hell were you?" Elaine asked, barely trying to mask her frustrated tone.

"Ah, sorry, ma'am," Marko said half-heartedly. "Had a bit of a bathroom emergency. You know how it is. Ate something I shouldn't have for lunch."

"Marko, I swear to God…" Elaine swallowed the threat that she was about to unleash, instead opting for a simple question. "Do you understand the heart attack you almost gave me? Do you have *any* idea what you just made yourself look like? Why didn't you notify us?"

"Sorry, sorry, it won't happen again."

Elaine snorted. "Yes, fine. Well, I guess we have the answer to that question." As well as the identity of our assassin. Possibly. "Looks like we're going to have to wait until Morris wakes up before we get any more information. End the lockdown. Anyone who's shift has ended during the investigation can go home. I'll stick around and question Morris myself when she decides to join us in the World of the Living."

About fifteen minutes later, Morris finally stirred.

"Good morning, Sunshine," Elaine said in a mildly sarcastic tone. "Nice of you to join us."

"Ugh, my eyes are burning and my head is killing me," Jolene murmured, seemingly still half-asleep. "Where am I?"

"You're in a holding cell in the detention center," Elaine said, seated in a chair facing the opposite direction, leaning her chin against the back of the chair. "Don't try to move. You're cuffed to your seat for safety reasons. Can't have you try anything ill-advised, now."

"Wait, what have you done to me?" Morris said, eyes widening.

Is that...panic? Elaine thought to herself.

"This is a violation of my rights!" Morris persisted. "I don't even know what I did. You can't just smack me around and hold me without reason, you know?"

Don't even know what you did? Bitch, you tried to kill me!

Her panic did seem pretty genuine, though. Elaine decided to press further.

"Wait, do you really not remember what happened?" Elaine certainly didn't believe her when she said it, but she wanted to see where this went. "Walk me through everything that happened from the beginning of your shift to right now. I want to hear it from your perspective."

"I...I'm not sure," she stammered. "It's all a blur. I came in, did some paperwork, and then...there's just a huge blank. The last thing I remember was...hearing about Jill." She gasped as the sentence left her mouth, as if she herself hadn't expected it. "Oh, God, Jill..." she sulked, sinking deeper into her seat. Reflexively, her arms moved, as if to wrap themselves around her legs as she slipped into a fetal position, but when her cuffed arms refused to move from their location behind her back, she relented.

"So it wasn't you?" Elaine asked, her tone softening a bit. *Looks like it may be time for Good Cop to come out. Damn. Should have brought in backup, but I guess I'll have to manage.*

The grief flashed to anger for a second. "What do you mean? Of course it wasn't me! I could never hurt Jill like that!"

Okay, I believe her a bit more now, Elaine thought to herself. *Let's keep pushing and see what we get.*

"Were you close?" Elaine asked, hoping to soften things before they escalated again.

"She was basically my older sister," Morris sighed. "It's all in my personnel file."

"I'd know that if I could access the damn thing," Elaine said. *Here's some bait. Let's see if you take it.*

"Why wouldn't you be able to access my personnel file?" Morris asked in a doubtful tone. "Surely that's one luxury that's afforded to you as a lieutenant, or whatever your rank is." The last bit was said with less of a ton of disrespect and more of a tone of legitimate uncertainty.

"No, you were right," Elaine said, reassuringly as she could. "And you're not wrong about my rights and privileges as a lieutenant. The problem, however, is the fact that the system is down, and apparently offline access to personnel files is just not something our force is bothering with."

All Morris could muster was a mild, "Oh."

Elaine looked the young woman over. She had to be only twenty, if that old. She still looked like a teenager. If Elaine hadn't known any better she would have put her closer to fifteen.

"Do you remember *anything* else?" Elaine pushed, trying to coax something, *anything* out of the poor woman, expecting nothing but swearing gratitude to the gods if she got anything.

"Nothing. Bits and pieces, I guess, but nothing reliable. I'm not sure I could even describe them to you let alone make sense of them."

"Not even the part where you shot at me?" Elaine pushed, trying to mask her frustration as much as she could.

Morris just shook her head. "I don't remember anything about that. Everything after a certain point is just a blur. I remember sadness and anger, but not why, beyond Jill being dead."

Elaine scowled. *Bless her heart she isn't making this any easier.*

One thing was making itself clear: this girl hadn't killed Jill. Why she decided to attack Elaine was another question entirely, but not one she was going to get an answer to any time soon, especially if she couldn't remember attacking Elaine in the first place.

Then something else dawned on Elaine. If this girl was supposed to get Elaine out of the way for somebody, it wouldn't take them very long to figure out that she had failed and they would probably be back for her. And since nobody knew who was responsible the first time, they certainly would be able to guess every precaution Elaine and the rest of the police would take.

Well, almost every precaution.

Elaine walked over to Morris' seat and released her cuffs. "Jolene Morris, I'm taking you into protective custody. Call it a hunch, call me crazy, whatever, something tells me I need to get you out of here. Now."

Elaine's communicator beeped as an incoming message was received. She had almost forgotten about the call with Brad. Surely he would be wondering why she wasn't responding, so she quickly read the message, silently thanking God that *that* function on her communicator was still working. At least the colony's network was more reliable than the police station's.

Elaine! Call me! Send a message! Start a damn smoke signal! Just SOMETHING to let me know that you're okay!

Elaine's mouth formed a tiny smile. *Jeez, Brad, keep your shirt on. It's not like I'm dead. Just almost dead.*

She quickly sent off her response.

Hey Brad, sorry for the radio silence. I'm fine now. Uh...a lot's happened and I don't have time to explain. I'm also going to be AFK for a bit, but don't panic. I'll see you soon.

"Okay, let's go." She grabbed Morris by the wrist and started towards the exit.

Chapter 7

Brad looked at the message in disbelief. Cortez was dead, and now Elaine apparently had some secrets that she couldn't just tell Brad over messages. Brad's assailant was likely not far behind, depending on how long it would take him to regain consciousness, and he probably wasn't in a good mood after the critical hit Brad dealt to him.

What time was it again? Mid afternoon sometime, like 2 or 3? Seems a little early for everything to fall apart. Brad usually waited for at least 4 or 5 PM before he let everything start on fire. Preferably even later, after dark so he could at least *enjoy* the pyrotechnics.

I gotta find somewhere to duck into so I can hide, at least for a little while.

Brad reached into his pocket to double-check that the hard drive was still there. He breathed a sigh of belief, noting that it hadn't slipped out during the scuffle. He then started jogging in a random direction, away from Cortez's apartment.

That was step one. Get the hell out of dodge. Where to? It didn't matter, just somewhere not there.

Brad slipped into a nearby bar, opting to take a corner seat. He took a look at his communicator and fired back a quick response to Elaine, hoping to get something back..

Okay what's going on? Why can't you just tell me now?

Minutes ticked by. Eventually it became clear that Elaine wasn't going to respond for some reason. Brad decided to scroll through the news, stopping on a developing story about a lockdown at the detention center. The lockdown had ended, but no explanation was available to journalists at this time, only that the on-duty lieutenant had slipped off to work on another developing case once the doors were unlocked.

Okay, but that doesn't explain why I can't get ahold of Elaine. She slipped out. Great. Why won't she respond?

Brad paused to think for a moment to try to get into Elaine's head. The only reason she would do something like this is if she didn't think she could take the time to chat about it. She wasn't much for keeping secrets. No, the obvious solution—besides her randomly deciding that she couldn't trust Brad anymore—was that she was still in danger somehow.

Brad cursed at the thought. Also at his own inability to help.

I guess I've got nothing to do but wait. Hopefully my stalker gets bored and calls off the hunt. Maybe he'll go trash my office instead.

As Elaine and Morris—Jolene, Elaine decided she should probably just call the girl by her first name at this point—walked the streets of the colony, eventually Jolene broke the silence.

"Where are you taking me?" she asked. "And you can let go of my arm, I'm not a child, and I'm not going to run away. I wouldn't know where to go even if I did."

Elaine had scarcely realized that she had even kept a grip on Jolene's arm. She obliged the girl's request, releasing her, poised to tackle her if she tried anything reckless. Which she did not.

"Thank you," the girl said, her sudden edge seemingly disappearing. "I'm sorry, I'm just a bit overwhelmed. It's...a lot."

Elaine quickly replied, "No, I'm sorry. I...kinda get like this. Tunnel vision. Hyperfocusing on one thing or goal. I really need to be more mindful of how I treat others when I have a lot on my mind. And I'm...still working out where I'm taking you, to be honest."

"So you're kidnapping me?" Jolene spat back.

"Of course not! You can go anytime, wherever you want, but I really think you're in danger." *Honesty is the best policy, after all.*

"Why do you think I'm in danger?" Jolene asked, clearly in disbelief.

"Look, you don't remember but you tried to kill me earlier today. As you can see, I'm still here, so whoever is behind your sudden temporary turn to the Dark Side is going to be *pissed* and they'll be back. I don't want to leave you alone to just get devoured by whatever they send after you. Enough people have already died for whatever the hell is going on here." There was a tinge of irritation in Elaine's voice, which she quickly offered an, "I'm sorry," for before continuing.

"Look, I promise I'll tell you everything when we get somewhere where I don't have to worry about looking over my damn shoulder every three seconds. Fair?"

Jolene raised an eyebrow before immediately letting her expression relax, relenting with a returned, "Fair."

Elaine smiled. "Excellent. Now, for the part you might not like as much. Turn off your communicator. Just for a little bit, okay. I want to make sure we're not being tracked or recorded. Don't worry, I know where we can drop our communicators for just a little while while we sort this out, all right?"

—

Hours passed before Brad felt daring enough to leave the tavern. To keep his nerves he just took nonalcoholic drinks. As much as he wanted to take the edge off, this was one of the few times when the edge was the exact thing he needed. However, the occasional soda would suffice. Just enough to keep him from getting thrown out of the establishment for loitering. Just enough to not look *completely* suspicious or paranoid as he constantly checked the door as it opened, just waiting for his stalker to make an appearance.

After one hour of this, he let his guard down a little.

After two hours, he stopped checking the door so frequently.

After three hours, he felt comfortable enough to leave his seat.

Finally, after four hours, he settled his tab, which was significantly more expensive than he had planned for this evening, and walked out the door.

He tried to contact Elaine once again, only this time receiving the notification that the user was unable to be reached, meaning her communicator was switched off. Hopefully. Hopefully the line itself wasn't disconnected.

Okay, where to now?

Brad needed to have the hard drive examined, so he quickly shot a message out towards an old "acquaintance" of his.

Not long after Brad had arrived on the colony, one of his first contracts was for a woman named Sonia Chambers, a computer programmer who had joined the colony with one of the founding corporations. Sonia had gotten fired from her post following accusations of abusing a programming error to embezzle thousands of credits from the company's account. It wasn't a particularly cheery case. She was totally innocent, and it turned out that her supervisor was behind the whole thing, setting Sonia up to take the fall for her. There wasn't sufficient evidence to convict Sonia, which kept her out of prison. However, there wasn't sufficient evidence to convict her supervisor either. Eventually said supervisor skipped the colony and the company went under due to the loss, which was on top of the already extreme investment inherent to starting the colony in the beginning.

Sonia was able to find freelance programming work to keep herself employed, but the loss of such a lucrative position following the company's failure was a sore spot, and she likely wouldn't respond well to the sudden contact from Brad.

The message was simple. "Hey, it's Brad. I need some tech help. I'll pay."

Before too long, a voice call rang over his communicator from Sonia. Brad answered, trying to hide any uncertainty in his voice.

"Hey, Sonia..."

Sonia's curt voice snapped back, "You've got a lot of nerve 'Hey Sonia'ing me. What do you want?"

"Okay okay, I'll cut straight to the chase. Vince and Jill Cortez are dead, and I've got a hard drive that has some information that people really seem keen to keep under wraps."

"Okay Asher, slow down. First off, what? Secondly, who?"

"Look, I can explain when I get there. I'm still trying to process everything myself. Can we please just set up a meeting?"

The line went silent for a few seconds, before Brad frantically shouted, "Hello?!"

"Calm down, I didn't hang up on you. Try to swing by my office this evening...say...8 o'clock?"

Brad quickly checked the time. That would give him about two hours. Just long enough for him to swing by his own office and try to get all of his information organized. "Yeah, that should work. I'll try not to get followed."

"What are you—you know what, never mind. You better make this worth my while." And with that, she ended the call.

Well, the clock's ticking. I better get back to the office.

Brad wasn't sure what he was expecting to see when he got back to his office, but seeing Elaine sitting by the door with her arm in a sling sitting by another, younger officer wasn't on the list.

"Elaine!" Brad shouted, rushing to her side. "Why are you here? Why haven't you answered my calls or messages? What's up with your *arm?*" He looked at the other officer. "And who is this?"

"It's a long story. Can you let us in so we can lock the door and sit down for a bit? Also do you happen to have any ibuprofen? Or liquor? This arm is killing me."

"Yeah, hang on." Brad fumbled with his keys, opening the old glass door that originally came with the building. Once everyone was seated and the door freshly locked, Brad asked if his guests wanted any food. Not that he had much to offer, but let it never be said that Brad Asher didn't *try* to be a good host.

"This is Officer Jolene Morris," Elaine began. "She's relatively new to the force here, but wouldn't you know it, she's already got assault and attempted murder of another officer of the law under her belt."

Jolene opened her mouth. "You keep saying that, but I don't remember any of it. What about your own use of excessive force? Maybe that could explain my amnesia."

Elaine shot a glare back in Jolene's direction, but she tried to keep it professional. "Look, I didn't do anything to your head, so whatever caused your little bout of amnesia happened before our little scuffle. You're damn lucky I didn't just gun you down after the first shots—yours, mind you—were fired."

"Well you didn't, and it's too late for that, so kindly bite me." Brad almost imagined the young woman sticking out her tongue at Elaine.

"Ladies, ladies, let's back up a bit," Brad pleaded. "Now, why were you trying to kill Elaine?"

Jolene quickly responded, "I'll tell you again like I keep telling her, I don't remember doing anything of the sort."

Elaine sighed. "She really doesn't seem to remember it. It's like an entire chunk of the day was just erased from her memory somehow. That's what she told me, and in my defense—" she glared at Jolene again, "I *do* believe you. It's just that it's a little convenient, is all I'm saying. And that usually means trouble."

"Trouble?" Brad asked, his question answered by a nod from Elaine.

"Yeah, that's why I have her with us. She can't surprise me if I don't let her leave my sight, though more importantly...I think someone might be after her next."

"Okay, this is a lot all at once, let's tackle this one topic at a time. So it wasn't under anyone's orders?" Brad butted in, hoping to steer the conversation away from the world's most uncomfortable cat fight going down in the middle of his office.

Jolene paused for a second, and then said, "If it was, I sure don't remember it. I'm sorry. I wish I had more to offer, but this whole day has been a bit of a blur."

"Yeah, that's what she keeps saying," Elaine said, as if to corroborate the girl's testimony. "Has anything come back to you since we left the police department?" she then asked Jolene.

"I...I don't know."

Brad, watching the exchange go back and forth like he was trying to judge an extremely tense tennis match on the razor's edge of devolving into a brawl, noticed something on Jolene's neck. A small puncture wound, marked by a tiny dot of dried blood. A wound that wouldn't have drawn much blood, probably wouldn't have even hurt that much if she wasn't aware of it, but perhaps could have been large enough for a syringe of some kind.

"Hey, Jolene, what happened to your neck?" Brad asked, stepping forward to get a closer look.

"My neck? What do you mean?" She felt around for the wound, flinching when she found the pinprick. "Ouch, that's a little tender for some reason. That the place?"

"That might explain the sudden snap to violence. Let's start from the top. Try to remember *anything* you can," Brad suggested in a hopeful tone.

"You mean you really don't know where the cut on your neck came from? I mean, I guess I hadn't noticed it before now but it's definitely there." Elaine said, edging closer.

"No," Jolene began, "Honestly, like I keep saying everything from the beginning of my shift to when I woke up after you'd apprehended me is a bit of a blur. I figured that was just because of how upset I was at Jill's death."

"Upset enough to unilaterally try to kill the person you thought was at fault without proof?" Elaine muttered before holding up a hand as Brad glared at her.

"Yeah, about that," Brad broke in, before the shouting match could continue, "what's your relationship with Jill? I mean, it seems like she was really important to you."

"Oh, right..." Jolene looked at the floor sadly. "She was kind of like a big sister to me. My family on Earth isn't particularly well off. It was just me and my siblings. Dad was gone most of our childhood, and Mom died when I was a teenager."

"Yeah, that sounds pretty typical," Brad muttered before thinking to himself, *Hell, you still look like a teenager. How old are you?*

—

Life on earth was, to put it lightly, extremely divided between two vastly different economic castes. One was born either incredibly wealthy, living in nice, well-kept cities, usually built above older, more run-down neighborhoods that were frequented by those unfortunate enough to have been born lower class, poverty-stricken people who, barring the few formerly of the upper class who blew their fortunes on drugs, gambling, and other forms of "slumming it", tended to be stranded not far from their original places of birth.

Any middle class citizens who found themselves unable to break into the upper echelons of Earth society due to the prohibitive cost of living in the newer, typically safer cities usually would make their way towards the stars. Lunar colonies tended to be the most rich in opportunity. A solid silver medal that could be found more or less in Earth's own backyard for those who were willing to put in the effort and make the sacrifice.

The quality of life expected from colonies decreased as distance from Earth increased. Without much of the groundwork already accomplished by colonists' predecessors, there was an inherent risk to volunteering for such colonial expeditions. The kind of risk that was only really considered by volunteers that were either too brave, stupid, or desperate to try other avenues. Drugs and violence were the norm, and any sort of police work on these distant colonies tended to have a relatively high turnaround as the local sheriff, for lack of a better term, would either get fed up with the work and quit, or find themselves in a ditch due to their actions offending someone.

The Epiphany Colony, due to its location in orbit around Mars, was kind of in the middle as far as quality of life was concerned. Not on the bleeding edge of frontier exploration, but not so developed to be the next hot spot for the wealthier middle class in the Earth Federation. Maybe in another fifty years or so things would be different, but it wasn't something Brad was counting on.

—

"Anyway, we were taken in by Jill's family, up to the Copernicus colony."

Brad nodded. His family hailed from a lunar colony as well, so Brad was familiar with the names of the other colonies such as

Copernicus, even though he had never been there personally.

"Although, by this point I was close enough to adulthood that I was going to join a colony out in the direction of Saturn. Not that I had a particular job lined up, but I was sure I could land something with a research crew. Maintenance, construction, security, something like that anyway. The only thing that stopped me was Jill encouraging me to see if I could join the academy. She put in a good word for me as a reference, both for the academy and for my assignment here. Honestly, I kinda owe her family in general but her in particular everything." She looked at the floor, not wanting to show how even vocalizing that thought hurt.

Elaine, whose posture relaxed somewhat while Jolene was talking, then said, "I guess I do remember Cortez mentioning someone being taken in by her family. Why in particular did they pick you over the legions of other cases just like you in the slums on Earth, though? It seems like a little much for a charity case." Brad shot another glare at Elaine, but said nothing.

If Jolene was offended by the charity case comment, she didn't show it. "I'm not really sure. I guess her father frequented a restaurant owned by my grandparents or something. Some connection there, anyway."

Brad nodded in understanding. "So Jill helps you get this job and even gets you assigned to the same precinct. She dies. Somehow you get it in your head that Elaine is at fault. Somewhere along the way, you decide Elaine has to die. I think the thing we're missing here is the why.

Jolene looked at her hands. "It's...not like that. I already told you everything I can remember. At some point I passed by the front desk and everything after is just blank."

"Did you talk to anyone there?" Elaine asked, leaning forward. "You hadn't mentioned that detail before. Are you remembering things?"

Jolene rubbed her temples. "I dunno. There was the receptionist. She was talking to...gah, I can't remember his name! I've been here a month, I should at least have the important people's names down! He's the captain that was on duty today."

Elaine sat up straight. "Captain? That doesn't sound right. I was the highest ranking officer on duty in the detention center today. I made the assignment myself to make sure Cortez would be safe."

"I don't know what to tell you. Maybe he was beginning his shift when things started to get hairy?" Jolene suggested. "It was getting close to shift change when...whatever happened happened, anyway."

"What did he look like?" Elaine asked. "Details. Anything at all you can remember."

"Uh...tall, dark hair, really tan skin. Asian. Middle-aged, maybe like...forties or fifties? In good shape, though, like he plays sports in his free time," Jolene rattled off. "I'm sorry, that's all I can piece together."

"Matsumoto? Shoji Matsumoto? Does that name ring a bell?" Elaine pressed, not willing to just give up on this potential lead.

"Ah yeah, that sounds right!" Jolene said, her face lightening up. "Yeah, I remember meeting him one time and seeing him around but I was usually on different shifts from him."

"Did you say anything to Captain Matsumoto?" Brad asked. "Did he say anything to you? Or, anything you can remember, at any rate?"

"I can't really remember. That's when things start to get blurry. Like, Jill's death was announced, and before I knew it, I was standing in her cell about to shoot Elaine." She rubbed her forehead. "I guess I do remember that part, now. I'm...sorry, I don't know what must have come over me," Jolene apologized, looking at the floor again.

Brad and Elaine looked at each other. "Drugged." They both said.

"Drugging makes sense," Brad continued, folding his arms. "If someone needed something done and needed an easy fall guy, that would probably be the way to do it. And now I think I get why Elaine has you with her. I can't imagine whoever tried to get rid of Elaine will be too happy to know that you failed them." Brad then changed the subject. "Do you know anything about Matsumoto?" He looked at Elaine expectantly.

"Not really. I've never worked alongside him, and he seems to really keep to himself. You don't think..." Elaine's expression filled in the blank.

"I really hope not," Brad answered, not needing to hear the rest of the question. "I suppose we'll figure that out with this." Brad pulled the hard drive out of his pocket.

"Oh yeah, what did you find?" Elaine asked. "I'm guessing you never were able to tell me how that whole thing went."

"I haven't been able to get into it. Yet. But I know someone who can, and I'm going to be meeting her later this evening. God willing, I might actually get out without getting yelled at this time."

Chapter 8

"**B**y the way, Elaine, what are we gonna do about your shoulder?" Brad asked. "That can't feel that great, and you probably can't do much with it."

Elaine rolled her eyes. "Oh, no, I'm fine. It's only a dislocated shoulder. No need to show that much concern," she muttered dryly. "I could go for something to drink though. Something to lighten the load, soften the edge, y'know? Oh, but I guess I shouldn't if we're going to meet your hacker friend."

"I dunno," Brad began. "I'm worried that if something happened, your injury could get worse. Maybe you better sit this one out, Elaine."

"Oh no you don't, Brad," Elaine began, poking Brad in the chest with her good hand. "Don't think for one *second* you're leaving me behind when you know as well as anyone else does that I can kick your ass all the way back to Earth with just one arm. Don't deny it."

"Ow, ow, okay, stop it, you're right. I just don't want you to get hurt." Brad looked away. "I mean, I don't know what I'd do if you got hurt because of a dumb decision I made."

Elaine playfully punched his arm. "Oh relax. If I get hurt because of someone's dumb decisions, I've got plenty of my own that I can blame. If anything you might be able to *stop* me from making some of those dumb decisions. Although you might also get yourself hurt without me there to bail your sorry butt out so it could go either way."

Damn, the girl drives a hard bargain. "All right," Brad relented, before adding, "but listen, the *second* things start looking sketchy, you get the hell out of there. This is a non-negotiable condition for this agreement."

Elaine raised an eyebrow. "Non-negotiable? Are you prepared to back that stance up? Or have you forgotten the previously-mentioned ass-kicking that I promised you?"

"I'm being serious," Brad stated firmly. "Threaten me all you want, it's the truth. I don't want you to get hurt."

Elaine chuckled, "You've never had much of a sense of humor. Fine." She raised her right hand to the square. "I solemnly swear that if things get sketchy, I will get the hell out of there." Upon seeing Brad's unamused expression, she winked. "Only if you promise to do the same, though."

"I said non-negotiable!" Brad fired back defensively.

"And this condition is my non-negotiable response to your non-negotiable condition!" Elaine playfully retorted. "C'mon, Brad. Please? For me?"

"Gah!" Brad spat in frustration. "Fine! You want it, you've got it."

"Good."

"You really should stay back and rest," Jolene said, finally breaking her silence. "If it makes you feel better, I'll go with Mr. Asher."

"You're hurt too, you know," Elaine fired back defiantly. "I mean, that stun gun plus the pepper spray can't have been good for you. Or has your headache already gone?"

"I guarantee I'm less hurt than you right now. You probably aren't even a decent shot with your shoulder like that," Jolene responded, unconvinced by Elaine's point. "A headache isn't quite as bad as a bum shoulder and you know it?"

"Oh yeah, what's your average at the range?" Elaine asked, smugly. "Should we have a little contest?"

"My average doesn't matter any more than yours right now against moving, armed targets. The fact is you're injured and would probably slow us down." Jolene then grinned. "But I'm willing to take you up on your little challenge when you're better. Loser buys lunch for a week?"

"Bring it!" Elaine exclaimed.

Brad broke in, "All right, ladies, calm down. Let's stay in the present for the time being. Trust me on this one, Jolene. It'll be better if we bring Elaine with us. We won't hear the end of it otherwise."

Elaine opened her mouth to say something, but then stopped herself. "I...yeah that's accurate."

"Do I ever miss?" Brad asked, with a grin. Elaine folded her arms, unamused.

—

As the time of the appointment drew near, the three of them set off for the building Brad playfully referred to as Sonia's secret lair. As they walked, Brad meekly requested that they not pass judgment on Sonia's digs, knowing that she would likely tear all their heads off if she felt the least bit insulted.

Jolene looked Brad over. She wasn't quite sure how he and Elaine had become friends. They seemed to be a strange pair, Elaine being so loud and outspoken while Brad seemed to be a bit more reserved. Eventually Jolene decided to ask some questions.

"So...where are you from, exactly, Mr. Asher?"

Brad seemed surprised at the question, or at least at the way he was addressed, because he quickly replied, "Just Brad is fine. Anyway, my family is on one of the lunar colonies, Serenitatis. Named for Mare Serenitatis, or the Sea of Serenity."

"Oh, so your family is rich, then?" Jolene winced. Probably should have worded that more tactfully. He might get defensive.

"Well, I guess you could say that. It's not like we had a butler or anything. Just a summer home in the Sea of Tranquility." Quickly spotting Jolene's glare of disbelief. "I'm kidding, I'm kidding. No, my dad works for a security firm on Serenitatis, big contract, all the cameras and alarms and such are his domain, and my mom's a doctor. So I'd be lying if I said we were destitute or anything like that."

"Look at you, leaving out the bit where you had a nanny," Elaine said playfully.

"Yeah, if by 'nanny' you mean older brothers, then sure, I guess," Brad said dismissively.

"And you're a private detective on some backwater colony out here in the boonies," Jolene continued flatly. "I'm not really sure how that works."

"Yeah, you could say that things haven't exactly panned out the way my parents would have wanted," Brad said wistfully. "To be honest, they haven't even panned out the way *I* would have wanted them to."

"What do you mean?" Jolene pushed.

"Mom wanted me to get into med school and become a doctor just like her. Hell, of the four of us, I'm the only one who hasn't ended up in medicine or Dad's security firm." By this point, they had stopped walking and Brad leaned against a wall, looking upwards.

Elaine broke in, "Yeah, his siblings were a lot more enthusiastic about the family businesses than Brad was."

"What happened, if you don't mind my asking?" Jolene inquired.

"I was always kinda the dumb one in our family. I mean, security didn't really interest me so that was never in the cards. Yes I see the irony. But I mean I tried. I went to a decent university. I majored in public health and minored in sociology. I wasn't a *terrible* student, and I did *fine* on all my exams, but I just never ended up getting accepted into a medical program I was happy with. Before I knew it I was just working nights as a shopping center security agent." Brad sighed. "That part was the worst. I still struggle to keep a regular daytime schedule, to be honest."

"Why didn't you keep applying to different medical programs?" Jolene asked, her interest piqued.

"The truth is..." Brad paused, trying to consider his words. "I was only really going into medicine because I didn't think I had any other options. That somehow my life wouldn't be seen as successful if I wasn't in some prestigious profession like my parents. I didn't bother taking any career aptitude tests because I wasn't sure I'd find something that would be a better fit because of what I already knew growing up."

Jolene grimaced. "That hardly seems fair."

Brad turned toward Jolene. "What do you mean?"

"It's just...I didn't have many of the same opportunities that you did. It sounds like you squandered a lot of the opportunities you did have."

Brad stood in silence for a bit, causing Jolene to cup her hands over her mouth in embarrassment. That coupled with Elaine's raised eyebrow made Jolene wonder if she should have said that.

"Y'know, you're not wrong," Brad admitted after an agonizing amount of time.

Elaine and Jolene said, "What?" simultaneously before looking at each other in amazement that they were on the same page.

"I did squander my opportunities. I wasn't exactly passionate about the idea of going into medicine and I wasted a lot of time in pursuit of something that I had no reason to believe would make me happy or leave me fulfilled. I had opportunities that I took for granted, sure." Brad sighed again.

Jolene paused for a second. "I get the feeling there's a 'but' coming."

Brad nodded. "But by the same token, I think it's important to highlight the kind of pressure that I was under. At least, the pressure I *felt* like I was under. It may be an excuse, but it is important to know where I was mentally at the time."

"What do you mean?" Jolene asked, suddenly curious.

"Yeah," Elaine added. "This is all new to me so it's fascinating."

"My parents probably would have been fine if I'd decided to become a teacher or something else, but I was always too afraid to ask what they thought because I thought for sure they wouldn't approve of anything they considered 'less' or 'lower' than what they had done for their careers. Whether they're real or not, that kind of weighty expectation really does a number on people growing up."

"You know, you still could go for something like that if you wanted to," Jolene replied. When Brad looked in her direction, she added, "I mean, you're young. I had classmates in the academy that were much older than you. People change their careers at weird and different times of their lives. There's nothing wrong with that."

"I know. But the thing is...I don't think I want to anymore," Brad said, thoughtfully.

"Why?"

Brad smiled. "I like being my own boss and being able to say no to work I don't want to do. I know I don't seem like it considering I'm friends with Elaine but I kinda hate being told what to do, and I have a bit of a problem with authority." He chuckled, not acknowledging Elaine's defensive glare in his direction. "I mean, I might hate the fact that my family sees me as the screw-up, but that doesn't make it any less true. But there's something truly magical about being your own boss."

Jolene fell silent. She hadn't been expecting such a frank response. In truth, she had expected him to be more defensive, but he seemed totally fine with what she had to say, like he had already said it to himself so long ago.

Still, one question did remain.

"So how did you and Elaine become friends?"

Brad and Elaine looked at each other, and both started laughing. "Honestly, we were from the same colony growing up. Attended the same high school. Went to the same university. Had a few similar classes."

"Ah, that would explain why you two seem as close as you are. When she dragged me to your office she didn't explain why, just that it was the safest place she could think of. Is she the reason you moved here?"

Elaine sputtered, stammering a response, while Brad paused, trying to figure out how to put his thoughts to words.

"I mean, I guess. She'd heard that I wasn't doing so well and said I should try to become a police officer. How do you deal with it? I mean, you're so different, yet nothing she does seems to bother you.er out here. She said that it was full of opportunity. I personally didn't want to do any more school, but I thought I could at least open up a detective agency thanks to my experience from my security gig."

"She said there were a lot of opportunities here?" Jolene said, looking at Elaine doubtfully.

"Yeah, that she did," Brad said, though his tone and expression had what seemed to be a message of "ask me later", so Jolene decided to change the subject a little.

"You seem pretty impervious to whatever nonsense she pulls on you. Why is that?"

Brad grinned. "It's taken time but I've learned how to speak and understand her own language."

"Her...what?" Jolene asked, confused.

"It's a secret, but the truth is she just loves feeling needed. I'm not sure how healthy it is, and I couldn't tell you where it came from, but she's just not happy if she doesn't get a chance to help people. It's why she became a police officer in the first place. I just kind of let her do her thing because she clearly gets something from it. If we get out of this and you're able to try building a positive friendship with her, try letting her do something nice for you."

Elaine scowled. "You know I'm right here, right?"

Brad laughed again. "Yes I do. And you know I'm right, right?

Elaine opened her mouth to respond, however, she seemed to quickly change her mind and closed it again.

Jolene pondered this for a while. These two were clearly nuts.

Is this some rich person thing that she was just too poor to understand?

She paused at this thought. No, that's definitely not the case. True, people of all walks of life exist whose entire reason for being came down to serving others. Service towards others in general seemed to be something that most people found satisfaction in, but there were some people who, for some reason, felt it needed to be taken to an insane degree, that if they weren't spending every waking moment they could in the service of others, they couldn't find happiness or fulfillment. True, everyone likes to be needed, but for those who so dislike feeling unneeded that they lack the ability to just relax a bit, what is there to be done.

Jolene sighed. These people were clearly nuts.

"We're almost there," Brad said, causing Jolene to jolt back to reality. He indicated the building up ahead. An old net cafe? Like, one of those places where you could pay money to sit at a computer and access the local and extended networks of Earth and her surrounding colonies? "Sonia owns this place. She uses it as a front for her hacking and programming gigs. Just be polite and don't touch anything and maybe we'll get away without Sonia starting us ablaze. Sound good?"

Chapter 9

"You're late," Sonia snapped once Brad, Elaine, and Jolene entered the room she was using at the network cafe, completely without looking up from her computer. "What took you so long?" Sonia Chambers, a brunette in her mid forties, was not the typical Hollywood stereotype of the female computer programmer, with the mousy hair and coke bottle glasses, nor was she the heavily-pierced goth or punk rock archetype.

In fact, judging from her physique, you'd think she was a professional athlete. Which wouldn't be that far off, as her biggest hobby was basketball, something she took great pride in. In fact, Brad was pretty sure she would be a lot more personable towards him if he played a few rounds one-on-one with her, because she would assuredly absolutely destroy him.

Brad quickly responded, "Sorry, I kinda got held up."

"My fault," Jolene quickly added.

Sonia looked up from her computer to acknowledge Jolene,

before saying, "Who's the kid? Seems to be a little young for you."

Jolene piped up, "Kid? Ma'am, I'm 22 years old."

"Yeah, and Brad here's in his 30's."

"I am not! I've still got...umm..." Brad quickly did some math, "Thirteen months left!"

"Ah, my mistake, seven years' difference ain't so bad. About as much between me and my ex-husband."

"Look, I'm not dating either one of them," Brad said defensively.

Sonia shot a look at Elaine. "Is this true? It's okay, sweetie, you can tell me, I won't judge"

Elaine quickly broke eye contact. "No, it's true," she muttered.

"Yeah, whatever you say. So what am I doing for you?" Sonia asked, trying to hurry this along.

"Ah, right," Brad, caught up in the topic of his love life, had forgotten about the hard drive. He pulled the hard drive from his pocket and laid it on Sonia's desk. "I need what's on this hard drive."

Sonia looked at the drive, then back to Brad, saying in disbelief, "You want me to pull some files. Can't you do that?"

"Look, I tried to get into it before but I struck out with the password," Brad said, sheepishly.

"You struck out with the password? Sounds like a you problem. Why is this stuff so important anyway?" Sonia asked, staring right at Brad. It's like the woman knew just how to make Brad uncomfortable and was intent on capitalizing on it every chance she got.

"It's something people really want to keep under wraps. At least two people have died for this, possibly more. I think that's plenty. At any rate, do you want my money or not?" Brad hated this part of the dance with Sonia. Without outright saying it, Sonia seemed to enjoy berating Brad for not having an expected level of basic computer proficiency.

"Right, about that..." Sonia began, not looking up to notice Brad's grimace, knowing what comes next. "I'm gonna need a little extra to cover the risk. Dead journalist and police officer? Possibility of police corruption? Seems a great deal more complicated than your usual cases. I thought you didn't take murder cases."

"Yeah, so did I. I'm still questioning why I took the case. Best case scenario, we survive and people start asking me to investigate riskier things." Brad shook his head, still in mild disbelief at how everything has panned out so far.

"Like you wouldn't pawn the hard stuff off on me," Sonia muttered.

Brad glared at Sonia. "Hard stuff? I don't hear about you getting stuff thrown at you. Nobody knows I even work with you!"

Sonia grinned impishly. "So you're taking credit for my work?"

Crap, walked right into that one, Brad scolded himself.

"I guess if you put it that way. Would you rather me credit you in every case I subcontract with you, possible risk and all? From where I'm standing you've got a pretty sweet gig. I get all the bullseyes painted on my face, back, and whatever else my marks feel like targeting, and you get a paycheck for doing whatever it is you do here on a daily basis in the first place."

"Fine, fine, let me see what I can do," Sonia said, finally relenting, satisfied at fully ruffling Brad's feathers.

She immediately hooked the hard drive up to her computer using an external machine Brad had only seen in this location, finally able to see what the thing was actually for. He could only guess at what else she was doing, as he only recently learned just what parts looked like what when working with computers. While she was working, Sonia made a modest attempt at some small-talk. "You never answered my question, Brad."

Brad, who had been scanning news articles on his communicator, asked without looking up, "What question?"

"The girl. Where does she fit into all this? I'm guessing you didn't just take on a decently-armed intern," Sonia clarified. "I mean, you can barely swing my rates, so she definitely isn't a bodyguard."

"Ah, right, sorry, I guess I forgot. She's a pretty new officer. Kind of an adopted sister to Jill," Brad replied, still looking at his communicator.

Jolene piped up, "Yeah, it's…kind of a long story."

"Oh, so is she the one who hired you?" Sonia asked, feigning interest.

"Nope," Elaine replied. "That's me. It was more the police corruption angle than the death of a family member. All business, for me."

"Pretty much," Brad agreed. " Jolene kinda fell into our laps at the detention center. Kind of an unintended passenger in the ride."

Sonia stopped working and looked up from her monitor. "Excuse me?"

Brad looked up from his communicator, sat up straight, and quickly explained everything that had happened from what he could remember or gather from the discussions with Elaine and Jolene, with the two of them filling in the blanks, making corrections, and clearing things up.

"Hold on," Sonia said. "You mean to tell me that you brought her along even though she tried to kill Alicia or whatever her name is?"

"It's Elaine," Elaine said in a frustrated tone. "And...yeah, that's accurate. She was drugged."

"Even if I wasn't," Jolene broke in, "Mr. Asher let us all travel together. Don't you think that says something?"

"Stop calling me Mr. Asher," Brad asked, somewhat fatigued.

"Right, you wouldn't want him to feel old or anything," Sonia replied smugly.

Brad rolled his eyes. "Look, regardless, she failed and the people behind this aren't going to take that sitting down. She's in as deep as any of us."

"All right, it's your funeral." She continued working, eventually saying, "Well, I gotta hand it to you, Brad, you certainly knew the best time to stop trying to brute force the password. You were extremely close to triggering the failsafe and having all of the data wiped."

Guess that's one thing I'm gonna have to thank my stalker for.

She worked for a bit longer, and then said, "That's it, I think we have a winner. Just taking a brief look through the files, and he probably should have given the files less incriminating names. They're all shipping records, for a bunch of firearms, armor, and explosives by the look of things. Not purchased by a specific company, but through a name. Shoji Matsumoto. That can't be someone's real name, right?"

Brad looked at Jolene, whose complexion had gone a few shades more pale. "No, that's…definitely someone's real name. He's one of the police captains."

"Brad…don't credit me for this case if you get out of it alive."

"I don't get it, why is Captain Matsumoto's name on these documents?" Jolene asked, nervously. "Surely there's a mistake here. Or maybe it's all for the police department?"

"I mean, surely there's a planned project for expansion of the department, like equipment upgrades or something like that?"

"Oh, child," Sonia sighed. "I remember having that sort of naive faith once. And true, that would be the easiest explanation if not for one thing. If, like you said, he was ordering all this for the police department, sure, his signature would be on the shipping manifests, fine, but there would be some documentation of which specific precinct it was going to, with signatures from other government officials. I don't see anything of the sort here. No, these were purchased on a personal account. Where the hell he got the money for all this from is anyone's guess. Let's get a closer look at this shipping manifest. The dates for these all seem to be in the last couple months. That sucks. No chance of stopping them at this point, though maybe we could find wherever they're stashed."

Jolene frowned. Between this and the drugging—or whatever it was that happened earlier—it didn't seem real. As if she were no longer living a normal life but instead secretly the central character in a bizarre sort of reality show. She swore she saw something similar in a movie once.

It was all too much to process at once. Thankfully, Brad spoke up.

"If it's all here, I guess the big question is why I haven't seen an uptick in gun-related violence throughout the colony. And you guys are sure you haven't noticed anything of the sort either?" Brad asked Jolene and Elaine, his query met with shaken heads.

Sonia furrowed her brow. "Let's keep digging through these files to see if something else jumps out."
   Jolene suddenly wished she had her communication device. Perhaps some news sources had something to say about the construction.

She looked over at Brad, eyes firmly on his own communicator. *Oh, maybe he's already on it.* She edged closer to Brad, trying to look over his shoulder. Brad flinched as he noticed her sliding closer, before she awkwardly said, "Sorry, I was wondering if there was any news about construction projects. Didn't mean to be creepy."

Good save.

Brad's shoulders relaxed, and he said, "I'm looking and I don't really see anything."

"What do you know about Captain Matsumoto? Was he always involved with the police?" Brad asked after a stretch of silence.

Sonia stopped her search. "That's a good question. Might be worth trying to find his personnel file. I might take some time to sniff that out later. Why, though?"

"Never hurts to look," Brad suggested.

"This is getting too weird, too surreal," Jolene said, laying her head on her arms on the table.

Sonia leaned back in her chair and sighed. "Well, I reached the end of the files. If I'm being honest it just feels like I'm looking at some crazy person's conspiracy board as he hurriedly tries to explain what a Sasquatch is to me."

Brad pondered this statement, nodding. "We've got some stuff here, let's try to organize it. Guns where there probably shouldn't be guns, stashed somewhere on the colony. We know that they're not supposed to be here because Vincent and Jill Cortez had to die to keep that information from getting out, and chances are someone's going to be gunning for us next. So... does anyone feel like doing some snooping?"

Chapter 10

"I appreciate the enthusiasm, Brad," Sonia began. "But just where do you plan on starting? Among the three of you I can see two guns, neither meant to handle targets in body armor. Or do you think you're going to be able to use that kung-fu or breakdancing or whatever it is you do to dodge or catch bullets in flight?"

"Of course not!" Brad stammered, caught up in his own excitement for the next leg of the journey. "I mean...the girls have other stuff as well," he offered half-heartedly.

"Uh-huh," Sonia said, unconvinced, followed by a shrug from Elaine and Jolene. "I don't suppose you'd even know where to look."

"I mean," Elaine began somewhat defensively, "There's only so much space to hide stuff on the colony, including the docking bay. Get the information to the right people, and they'll only be able to hide it for so long, even better if we can find the cache ourselves."

"And what about defensive strategies?" Sonia pushed. "Look, I can get behind wanting to scope out the place before you turn everything over to the Feds or whatever it is your plan is, but I can't in good conscience let a bunch of kids run off half-cocked without a plan. And spare me your retort about being almost thirty," she continued when Brad opened his mouth, "When you get to be my age, most people are still kids to you."

"It's not like I want to be the center of this thing either," Brad muttered. "But it's going to be hard to turn what little information we have to the Feds and expect them to make a serious effort towards investigating it, especially since we can't really trust local police to not just bury what information we give them."

"You sure? It might be worth a try."

"What are we gonna do about Matsumoto, though? He's 100% the problem here," Elaine said, doubtfully.

"Well, what you have here might be enough to at least cause a localized controversy if it got leaked to the press. I mean, surely you kids know enough about your history to know how Al Capone got caught, right?" Sonia suggested.

"Sure, I mean, it was tax evasion, but what's that got to do with anything?" Brad asked, unconvinced.

"No, she's got a point," Jolene jumped in. "That was the smoking gun for everything else he was up to. The fact that he had the lifestyle he did without paying taxes or showing his income was what prompted the official investigation into all of his off-the-books dealings, and that might be an avenue that could work here."

Brad folded his arms. "Okay, that's fair, but I guess the next question is what do we do after? I mean, why hide such a big shipment of guns as a personal purchase? There couldn't be something big boiling under the surface here like an armed uprising, could there?" Brad asked, half-joking.

"Look, can we not joke about that?" Elaine said uncomfortably. "I don't like the idea of our colony joining some civil war movement against the Earth Federation."

"Me neither," Jolene agreed. "A lot of people would get hurt or killed over nothing. It's something I already experienced enough on Earth. So much violence, and all over trivial things.

Sonia's eyes narrowed, "Yes, thanks for that. Look, tell you what, say the word and this information goes out to the Feds as well as every news source I can put my finger on. That should at least be enough for the time being."

Brad paused to consider this. It was true. He could take this one shot and it would be over. He already won.

"Okay, do it. And Elaine, don't worry about payment for a while."

"No, I'm wiring you the money right now. Pay Sonia. It's only fair," Elaine responded curtly.

"You sure? I didn't do much," Brad replied sheepishly.

"You did exactly what I paid you for. I asked you to look into the death of my colleague's husband. You did just that. Take the damn money. I'm not going to take no for an answer," Elaine pushed.

"Yes, and I'm not running a charity here," Sonia said. "Pay up, Asher."

"All right, all right. Pleasure doing business with ya as always," Brad said flatly. "Thanks, Sonia."

Chapter 11

As the three of them left Sonia's office, Brad slid his hands into his pockets. Was this really supposed to be the way the investigation ended? Just find some information and tell the authorities, letting them handle it?

Naturally, Brad knew that the answer there was a resounding "Yes," after all, he had no real authority or jurisdiction on the colony when it came to solving and preventing actual crime, but something felt completely unsatisfying about the way things had panned out. He hadn't managed to find the person who actually pulled the trigger on Vincent and Jill Cortez. All he had discovered was that a local police captain was up to some shady stuff when off-duty.

Brad couldn't help but feel like there was something he had forgotten about.

As they rounded a corner, Brad was brought face to face with the answer to that question: his stalker, plus a handful of what Brad had presumed were his buddies. All armed with bats, clubs, and other such implements.

Brad, trying to hide his surprise, uttered a sarcastic, "Hi fellas. What can I do for ya?"

The man in the baseball cap that had attacked Brad earlier that day stepped forward. His face still covered in cuts and scratches looked extremely pitiful, as did the rush-job someone took to clean and dress the cuts. He spoke first, saying, "You've got something that belongs to us. We just want it back, is all. Just give it here and we'll leave you alone, no questions asked."

Brad scratched the back of his head. "I'm afraid I don't know what you're talking about," he said, playing dumb. "I don't have anything that doesn't belong to me, and even that doesn't include much.Though," he reached into his pocket, producing a crumpled business card. "I'm a detective, and I'm totally willing to help you guys find whatever it was you lost. I'll even give you the new client's discount!"

"Brad, let's just go," Elaine suggested, pulling his arm back the direction they came, before seeing another group closing in from that direction.

"Don't bother," the man in the baseball cap said. "You're not going anywhere. And besides, we just wanna talk. It's just one thing. I know you have it, Asher. I watched you leave the apartment with it."

"Oh, *that* thing," Brad said. "Yeah, that was mine. I lent it to Vince and I really needed to get it back. Jill gave me permission to spring it from their house. But I have some bad news. Sorry, I kinda lost it. I was kinda hoping maybe you'd know where it ended up."

"Are we really doing this?" the man said incredulously. "You see how many guys we have to your three. What we're asking of you isn't so hard. Just give us the hard drive, and we'll let you go."

"I don't know what to tell you, man," Brad said. "I don't have it." He turned his pockets inside out. "See? Gone. Now can I go? I'm missing my favorite show. You know how hard it is to avoid spoilers even with on-demand recordings, so please, beat it. If you really can't find it, call me and I'll happily give you my rates."

The man laughed. "So you don't have it. But I bet you know where it ended up. Maybe we'll just have to smack you around a bit, kinda loosen you up, then you'll tell us where it is and we can get it back. Or you can go get it yourself. Either way works for us really. Let's get him, boys!" He nodded in their direction and his buddies started closing in.

Elaine quickly drew her gun. "Stay back! I'm still a cop, you know, and so is Morris here." She turned to Jolene and whispered, "C'mon, back me up here."

Jolene snapped back to attention, "Uhh, right." She drew her gun as well.

The man laughed. "Go ahead. Take a few shots. I don't care. You don't have enough bullets to deal with all of us."

"If you wanna try it, be our guest," Elaine said, before muttering to Brad. "Grab the stun gun on the back of my belt. Trust me."

Brad muttered back, "What, the shotgun?"

"Trust me," she repeated.

Brad did as he was told, leveling the barrel at the group.

"Okay, that's a bit more of a surprise. So you aren't *completely* unprepared," the man said somewhat playfully. "Betcha don't have the guts to pull the trigger, though," he said, goading Brad.

The group in front of them broke into a run in Brad's direction.

Brad began to panic. This thing felt like a sawed-off shotgun, no way it could be classified as a stun gun. They got closer with each passing millisecond. Whatever time Brad had to make a decision had expired long ago, and Brad pulled the trigger.

The air in front of Brad exploded, and the recoil was fierce. Brad himself wasn't the most accustomed to using firearms, so upon seeing no blood he thought for sure he missed, even accounting for the spread of shotgun pellets. Regardless, three of the guys in the front of the group were knocked back by the force from the blast, while the others stopped in confusion as to what happened, clearly not having expected lethal force, nor were they expecting Elaine to have grabbed Brad and Jolene by the wrists, dashing forward through the opening that had just formed in their ranks.

The next several minutes were a blur of fists, bats, and shouting. The only thing Brad knew was that the path with the least resistance was the one right in front of him. Their only objective was to escape.

Brad was surprised at how good of a club the stun gun made up close. A quick thrust at one guy. A quick bash to the head of another guy. Brad had no idea how long it would take to recharge the blast, but he definitely could just keep swinging.

Naturally Elaine handled herself well, considering she had taught Brad a lot of what he knew about fighting. Her smaller frame and easy access to sensitive bits and cheapshots helped. As she had said long ago during one of their lessons, "A fair fight is fine for sport, but if you get in a fight in the real world, there are no rules. Gouge eyes. Kick shins and groins. Throw stuff. Use people as weapons against other people, if you're stronger than them."

Unfortunately the last bit wasn't coming into play as much considering Brad's own lack of physical strength. He gave one guy a good shove into another, but it didn't do much besides momentarily knock them off balance.

Brad heard another approach him from behind, letting out a huge breath of air as he lunged with his bat. Brad quickly ducked to the side, rolling his outside leg directly into the man's stomach. As he doubled over to catch his breath, Brad threw himself headfirst into the man's face, feeling a splatter of blood. Unfortunately, the impact stunned Brad as well. Thankfully their scuffle had attracted the attention of some local police officers, and before long a squad had descended on the brawl. Within seconds, Brad found himself in cuffs in the back of a police vehicle, with no idea where the others had ended up.

Chapter 12

The events of the last few hours went by at hyperspeed for Brad. A quick brawl breaking out on the colony was hardly out of the blue. In fact Brad himself had been given many a stern warning about his conduct when his previous marks had gotten too rowdy, usually by Elaine, but occasionally by other officers. As a result, Brad had certainly experienced the "other side" of the system, typically a couple hours to a night in the detention center, before or after the aforementioned dressing-down.

Normally this wouldn't have bothered him. It came with the job, as a clear slap on the wrist for drawing too much attention to the seedy underbelly of the colony, but because Brad had almost always been acting in self-defense, charges brought against him were negligible, as would probably be the case this time.

No, the knowledge that someone died in this building earlier that day was what had Brad concerned, especially since they hadn't been able to identify the killer and surveillance footage was just *gone*. The fact that it could happen *again* had Brad extremely worried.

Get ahold of yourself, man, Brad thought to himself. *Maybe they—whoever they are—will just write it off as something unrelated to the Cortez case.*

Thankfully whoever was in charge of the detention center that night had the common sense to keep Brad separated from his new buddies. Unfortunately Brad lost track of where the girls ended up during the scuffle, and not even the officers that brought Brad in knew where they were.

"Relax," a particularly rough, muscular officer began, "Your mommy won't have gotten too far."

"Is that a hint of jealousy I hear? It's not my fault she likes me more than whatever kind of livestock you are." After saying it Brad immediately winced, knowing that Elaine would have snapped at him for giving another cop that much lip.

The officer responded with an attempt at a casual curse in response, though Brad noticed a slight hint that his word had cut deeper than the officer let on. "Just know that I wouldn't be so merciful on your happy ass as she has been with all the trouble you've caused."

Brad grinned. It always felt nice to give the lunkier officers some attitude when he felt like he could get away with it, which wasn't often. "Yeah, I'll be sure to avoid getting beat up in the future. I know how much paperwork I cause you guys by being the victim of violent assault from people breaking the law and stuff like that. Can I go now?"

"Just tonight you broke one some guy's nose!" the officer fired back defensively.

"Yeah, and he and his buddies were armed and attempted to assault me, an innocent man, and two of Epiphany's Finest, but I noticed your compassion for them is notably dry." *I should probably stop poking the bear. His only crime was being annoying.*

The officer scoffed and left. Brad opted not to make another joke.

Instead, he found himself lying on the sparse cot in the holding cell, staring at the ceiling. *Jerks. Least they could have done is lend me some paper so I can outline my findings a bit better.*

Then again, if there was really a benefactor in the police force for whatever it was that was going on, Brad wasn't even sure how he was going to get out of the holding cell to put his findings to good use.

Captain Matsumoto was, if nothing else, at least a contact within the police for someone else to purchase a bunch of weapons and have them hidden away on the colony, for some purpose. Maybe transport elsewhere. Maybe dispersal into local gangs. Hell, maybe the guy just had a gun fetish, whatever it was, it was sketchy. And here Brad was, just hoping that he couldn't be tied to this investigation so he had a fighting chance of getting out of here without a bullet in his back or brain.

As he lay there, pondering his future, what little of it he felt was still there, he glanced at the door. Besides a small glass window in the top, one couldn't see what was going on outside the cell. The walls, as well, were of a type of glass whose transparency could be manipulated via an external switch. Brad thought it was really cool. It was usually opaque to preserve the privacy of the person held within, but the opacity could be decreased if multiple people had questions for them. Why the visitor's room wasn't also like this was something Brad never could get a straight answer about.

As he mused, the door slid open, and in walked a middle-aged Asian man in an impeccably neat police uniform. "Brad Asher, I presume? I don't believe we've met."

"You presume correctly," Brad said, not rising from his seat. "And I take it you're Captain Shoji Matsumoto, right?"

"You've done your homework," Matsumoto said with a chuckle.

"To what do I owe the pleasure?" Brad asked flatly.

"I'll cut to the chase. You have something I need." Matsumoto said bluntly. "I'd like it back, very much. And I would make it worth your while. Far more than whoever hired you to steal it in the first place. What's your rate? I'll double it."

"Gee, Cap," Brad said, "I dunno if my new friends in the other cells told you but I don't have it anymore, and I don't know where it ended up. I mean, I could tell you my rate, it is pretty steep, but unfortunately no amount of money you give me will make me be able to pull it out of my ass and give it to you. Wish I could but unfortunately them's the breaks."

Matsumoto showed no change of expression. "That's too bad," he began. "You see, if that were to get away from me, it would be most unfortunate."

"Can't help you there, man," Brad replied, his own expression not changing. "You sure one of my new buddies didn't steal it in the scuffle?"

"Afraid not," Matsumoto admitted. "But there were two other police officers spotted fleeing the scene by some eyewitnesses, your new friends included. You wouldn't happen to know anything about that, would you?"

"Nope, I was hoping you'd be able to answer that question, but *c'est la vie*." Brad sat up on the cot. "So...can I go?" he asked hesitantly.

"Unfortunately nobody has posted your bail, so no. It's high time you took responsibility for your antics here rather than getting bailed out by that friend of yours." Matsumoto looked at Brad firmly.

"Understood. Have a nice day," Brad said dismissively.

"Will do," Matsumoto said, leaving, before pausing in the doorway. "However, should you feel more...cooperative...do let the guard on duty know and I'll see what strings I can pull to make things go a little more quickly."

"Noted," Brad said flatly. He heard the door slide shut as Matsumoto left.

I dunno if I'm angry or impressed at how brazen he was. Probably screwed with the surveillance systems again to get a "private audience" with me. Well, nothing to do but wait, I guess.

—

When Elaine had heard the approach of the officers that arrested Brad and the thugs, she instinctively grabbed Jolene by the arm and ducked into an alleyway nearby. A tense few minutes passed as they waited for the scene to clear up. Once the officers had left with Brad and the thugs in custody, Jolene moved to speak, stopping when Elaine put a hand up.

"Let's get somewhere a little more quiet first. I know of a place," Elaine said softly.

Said place was a small coffee shop nearby, the same one that Elaine had left their communicators at before. As they entered, Elaine let out a quiet greeting to the person behind the counter, a middle-aged Hispanic woman who Jolene could only assume was the owner given her age. The woman led them to a small room separate from the main floor of the shop, the employee break room, no doubt, fully furnished with a viewscreen, a table, a few chairs, a couple lockers, and barely any room to stand or walk around. The kind of room Jolene had spent no small amount of time in previously working in a restaurant before she and her siblings were taken in by Jill's family.

"What's this about?" Jolene finally asked.

"Oh, I'm a regular here, and I talked her daughter out of

marrying some guy who was a bad match for her. She's now studying law somewhere closer to Earth, so they consider me family," Elaine explained.

"Yes," Coffee Shop Lady said, "Elaine has done a lot more than that, but regardless, she's family. I told her if she ever needed a place to hide out while working, my break room was always open to her. You can call me Leila. So who's your friend, Elaine?" the woman—Leila—asked, turning to Jolene.

"Oh, my name is Jolene Morris," Jolene replied.

"Another cop," Elaine said, already sucking down a cup of coffee that Jolene hadn't seen Elaine get. Seeing Jolene's confused expression, Elaine then said, "Oh, my bad, do you want one? My treat."

"No no no," Leila interrupted. "It's on the house and you know it. How do you like it?"

"Uh...cream and sugar, please," Jolene responded hesitantly, as Leila stepped out to grab a cup, the cream and sugar, and the coffee pot.

"Like I said," Elaine continued, smirking, "My treat. So what I get is technically free, big whoop."

"Always the jokester," Leila said. "If you need anything, just hollar. Or be like Elaine and just help yourself."

"Thanks as always," Elaine said. "Jokes aside, you have no idea how helpful this is right now."

"Anytime, chica," Leila said, waving a hand as she walked back to the front of the shop.

"So...what are we gonna do about Brad?" Jolene quickly asked once they were alone. "I wouldn't have expected you to just bail on him like that."

"You say that like it's something I *wanted* to do," Elaine said, folding her arms. "You were there, things kind of got away from us. But here's what we know now. Brad's going to be kept in the detention center for a short period of time, and because I'm not there to bail him out, it will probably be longer than normal."

"And what is normal?" Jolene broke in. "You mean this has happened before?"

"Eleven times, which considering his clientele is kind of impressive. Normally he'd be out in a couple hours with me there to speed things along, if even that. However, that's probably not going to happen now. And considering Matsumoto's probably still on duty cleaning up after...after I left my post, it's probably less likely he'll get out any time soon."

"Wait, if Matsumoto's still there, shouldn't you be worried something will happen?" Jolene asked frantically.

"I don't think he'd try anything so drastic if he even knows I hired Brad in the first place, but if he does, he might try to bribe Brad. But no, you're right, we're going to need to spring Brad eventually. But we're not going *anywhere* without a plan. Any ideas?" Elaine looked at Jolene hopefully.

"You could take me back to the station," Jolene suggested.

"Pardon?"

"Technically I'm still in police custody. You never *did* officially release me. You just unlocked my cuffs and dragged me out of the building," Jolene reminded Elaine.

"Oh yeah, paperwork and such," Elaine said. "In the heat of the moment, I kinda forgot about all that. But I don't know if that's gonna work."

"Why not?"

"I don't know if the cameras were back up when I left with you. If there's footage of me taking off with you in tow, that could be bad." Elaine rubbed her forehead. "Dammit, I made some dumb moves today."

"Just be honest," Jolene suggested. "Say you were worried for my safety and you thought I'd be safer in your custody, and just say we got jumped because of me."

"I thought you asked me to be honest," Elaine said flatly. "That last part was because of Brad."

"Details, details. Nobody knows the whole truth but us, and as far as anyone but the officers that arrested everyone know, I'm still dangerous." Jolene grinned, "I mean, I am, but not in the way they think."

"Okay, and what if that doesn't work?" Elaine asked, doubtfully.

"Well, do *you* have any better ideas?" Jolene responded defensively.

"Honestly...no. I don't know if the Trojan Horse thing will work, but I'm certainly willing to try it. We'll just have to wing it if it doesn't work."

God save us if it doesn't, Elaine thought, with Jolene's expression seeming to indicate a shared understanding.

Chapter 13

The lights in the cell dimmed, signaling night had completely fallen. Time to go to sleep like a well-behaved prisoner. Honestly, the fact that Brad had somehow lucked into getting his own cell made sleep feel just that much more appealing, but he had decided against it for the time being. Call it instinct or paranoia, but he was almost certain that, since he had in no uncertain terms rebuffed Matsumoto's offer, they might try intimidation as phase two of whatever their plan for him was. That was assuming Matsumoto had the class and decency to not just let an assassin in to kill him.

No, they would try to ruffle his feathers a bit, but without him around they would be back to square one as to where the hard drive was. Not that it mattered, since by now, if Sonia was on her A-game, all of that information would be flooding the nets. It would be the talk of the town, certainly, something that no one would be able to keep a lid on.

Hell, that might be what made up Matsumoto's mind.

Well, whatever they were going to do, they would likely wait to spring it on him after he had tried to go to sleep.

Brad grinned to himself. Time to spring the trap.

He spread himself across the cot. Not the worst thing Brad had tried to sleep on before, but it was far from what he would consider comfortable or even adequate for a decent night's sleep. Not that it mattered. Brad had no intention of sleeping. Though just how he responded would depend entirely on how many people Matsumoto sent in to "intimidate" Brad. He was sure he could take *one* thug, but they would definitely send more. Up to three was something Brad felt pretty sure about, but anything beyond three people would need a different strategy.

Brad took a look around the cell. Naturally he was out of luck as far as things he could *wield* to defend himself. Nowhere to hide either. He might be able to smash one guy's face into the cot or the wall if he *had* to. He hoped it wouldn't come to that.

Time to play the waiting game.

Brad lost track of time as he lay there, waiting, trying to feign sleep while also trying to *avoid* it, knowing full well that he was completely screwed if he fell asleep for real. To keep himself occupied, he tried to plan what he would do once he was out. Get a decent meal. Definitely get a shower. Maybe return to his office and just sleep for the next twelve hours.

As he mused about this, the steel door to the cell slid open. Brad, not looking directly at the door, waited for his visitor to identify himself. He certainly hadn't expected Matsumoto to make such a quick return, so when nobody spoke up but the footsteps slowly crept towards him, he moved his focus to the sounds of the steps. From the slow, regular rhythm of the taps as the feet touched the metal floor, Brad could deduce that either they were extremely well-coordinated, or it was a single guard. Feigning rolling over in his sleep, Brad tried to angle his view towards the door.

Sure enough, they'd just sent in one guy to intimidate him. He was about Brad's size, wearing an all black outfit with a scarf to hide his face. And he was confident, or at least it appeared, because nobody seemed to be watching from the door. Perhaps he had backup hiding close by, but Brad didn't have time to formulate a strategy for that.

Instead, he waited for the man to finish crossing the cell to his cot. Once the man had arrived at a satisfactory proximity to his target, he leaned forward as if to grab Brad. Brad opened his eyes wide, smiling, and delivered a hard punch under the man's chin, sending him reeling.

Wasting no time, Brad sprung to his feet, settling into a stance, saying, "It was nice of Matsumoto to send me someone to play with, but I'm afraid big, dumb, and confident isn't exactly my type."

The man seemed to take umbrage to that statement, as he immediately charged Brad to tackle him. Brad deftly lept aside, thinking to himself, *Okay, so he's trying to charge someone smaller and faster than him, but he's also smart enough to not have responded to that taunt verbally. Maybe I underestimated him just a smidge.*

As the man regained his footing, he turned to deliver a massive haymaker to Brad's face, faster than Brad had expected, as it clipped his cheek when Brad tried to dodge out of the way. The force sent Brad into a spin as he winced from the pain, knowing that a direct hit would probably have broken his nose. Brad tucked and rolled out of his tailspin, landing in a crouched position a few feet from the man. The man quickly closed the distance to tackle Brad to the ground. Brad smirked, seeing the opportunity. Putting his left arm above him to brace for the next move, Brad threw his right arm between the man's legs. The man instinctively jumped to avoid any form of testicular damage, and Brad used the man's momentum to flip him over himself onto his back.

At least, that was the plan, but Brad had forgotten about his cot nearby, which the man smashed into with his back, making a sickening crunch. The man shrieked in pain before falling limp.

Brad sat there in a confused awe for what felt like an eternity before he slunk closer to the man to check him. Feeling his neck, Brad found a pulse and breathed a sigh of relief that he didn't accidentally just kill a man. He quickly cast his eyes at the door. Nobody was standing there, despite the noise, but he wouldn't have much time until someone came to investigate. Brad started toward the cell's entrance before stopping himself.

No, if he's got buddies waiting in the wings, they might not take too kindly to me just strolling out. He looked at the man again, quickly mentally measuring him. *Then again, they won't question it if their buddy walks out, though I don't know what his speaking voice is like. Well, it's not like I have any other options.*

—

As Elaine closed in on the detention center, leading Jolene around the outer wall of the complex, she saw a group of people in black clothing standing at the entrance, as if they were waiting for something. Hoping they weren't spotted, Elaine and Jolene ducked behind the wall, peeking out to see what the fuss was all about. They definitely seemed to be waiting for someone, as there was a sudden surge of activity as another of their ranks ran out the front door. They all began to walk quickly towards the exit of the compound, talking.

"So what happened? You were in there a little longer than we planned," one of the masked men said to the one who had just left the building, startling him.

"I...uhh...that is...he put up a bit more of a fight than I expected. I hurt him pretty bad, though he might be more willing to negotiate with the boss when he wakes up," the man stammered.

"Careful!" the first man exclaimed, before saying something more softly that Elaine couldn't hear. Probably admonishing him for talking so loudly about "the boss", who could only have been Matsumoto.

"Ah, my bad, I'm just a little rattled is all," the newcomer continued, his voice sounding oddly familiar to Elaine.

"Ah come on, Leo, don't be such a baby. This isn't your first time putting pressure on someone and you know it, and I know you've done worse," one of the other guys said.

The first guy then added, "Your voice sounds a little weird, Leo. Are you sick or something?"

The newcomer stopped in what could only be seen as a panic. "Uh...yeah," he gave an attempt at a cough. "I think I'll be fine. Just a cold."

That guy is totally Brad, Elaine thought to herself, wondering if Jolene had put the dots together. *And I don't know if he's doing a convincing enough job of acting.*

As the group walked closer, "Leo" fell silent, which made Elaine more suspicious of his identity. She also caught herself praying that once they exited the detention center's compound, they'd turn the other direction and not see her and Jolene loitering outside the wall. Or if they did turn her direction, she wanted to avoid having them see her or Jolene's faces. With each step, Elaine prayed harder, *Turn left. Turn left. TURN LEFT.*

As they began to spill out of the wall, she quickly looked at her communicator, trying to act natural, as they turned right and walked right past her and Jolene.

Oh God, Brad, please don't call out to us, Elaine caught herself thinking before feeling guilty for doubting Brad's intelligence that much. He could be kind of a derp in public, but that didn't mean that he was dumb enough to out himself while in disguise...right...? She continued to "act natural" as the mob, about eight people all told, walked past.

She bit her lip in anger. She didn't get a good count of the number of the people that jumped them as they were leaving Sonia's place, but there could have been eight of them, and if these were the same guys, then Matsumoto just *let them go*, and it sounds like they immediately used their newfound freedom to try to rough Brad up. She was definitely going to have to give the boss a piece of her mind when she saw him next.

—

As Brad undressed the thug, he realized that this guy was one of the guys that jumped him outside of Sonia's place. He quickly dressed himself in the man's clothes, scarf included, wondering where he'd gotten the outfit so quickly. He'd only been in the detention center for a few hours, so unless there was a man on the inside just passing out thug uniforms that he'd missed, someone, likely Matsumoto, had sprung the gangsters, let them get changed, and then had them come back to "persuade" Brad to join ranks with them.

Brad spat on the ground of his cell. The nerve. Thankfully they hadn't armed the guy with much more than what he'd had before or else there could have been real trouble. Properly outfitted, Brad let himself out into the hallway, shutting the door to the cell behind him. He almost felt sorry for the poor lunkhead who attacked him, being abandoned in nothing but an embarrassing pair of tighty-whities in the police holding cell, but if he was really desperate he could borrow Brad's jeans and white shirt.

Brad was a little annoyed that he couldn't go back and get his jacket and other stuff as of yet—he had no idea where to even look for his stuff—but for the time being, he was going to have to just go along with whatever happened outside.

This annoyance turned to confusion as Brad looked up and down the halls of the detention center. There was *nobody* around. Sure, it was late at night and they likely only had a handful of people on staff, but where he expected to see one tired officer wandering the halls, he saw nothing.

As Brad sauntered through to the front exit, he finally found one guard, asleep at his desk. At least, Brad assumed he was asleep, as he was definitely breathing, and most certainly not paying attention to what was going on around him. Edging closer, Brad saw a dart sticking out of his neck.

They tranqued him. Makes sense, I guess.

Exiting the door, Brad found a small mob of seven other guys wearing the same outfit that he was. One among them spoke up with a voice that Brad recognized as the leader of the gang that jumped them before.

"It's about time, Leo, let's get moving!"

"Uhh, right," Brad said, following the group as they began to leave the compound.

"So what happened?" the leader continued. "You were in there a little longer than we planned."

Brad gulped, not wanting to answer. The more he spoke, the more likely they were going to see through his disguise. "I...

uhh...that is...he put up a bit more of a fight than I expected. I hurt him pretty bad, though he might be more willing to negotiate with the boss when he wakes up," Brad stammered. *Nice cover.*

"Careful!" the leader exclaimed, before edging closer to Brad, whispering, "Remember what I said about mentioning the boss in public?"

"Ah, my bad, I'm just a little rattled is all," Brad responded, before grimacing at his terrible attempt at acting.

"Ah come on, Leo, don't be such a baby," one of the other guys said in a tone that was apparently supposed to be encouraging. "This isn't your first time putting pressure on someone and you know it, and I know you've done worse."

The first guy then added, "Your voice sounds a little weird, Leo. You sick or something?"

CRAP!

"Uh...yeah," Brad stammered, offering an attempt at a cough. "I think I'll be fine. Just a cold."

I'm so screwed, I better stop talking.

As the group exited the compound, they took a right turn down the small thoroughfare outside the wall. As Brad rounded the corner he saw two female police officers standing there, looking at the communicator in one of their hands. As they got closer,

Brad recognized them as Elaine and Jolene, his heart fluttering at finally having some confirmation that they were all right. He almost tried to get their attention before stopping himself.

No, no, I can't blow my cover now.

As he walked past, he and Elaine locked eyes.

Damn it, not now. Please. Do. Not. Say. Anything. Just follow us.

Elaine quickly went back to her communicator, trying to "act natural", and Brad breathed a small sigh of relief.

Good, now let's see where the mob takes us.

Chapter 14

Once she was sure that the small mob had walked far enough away that they wouldn't notice that they were being tailed, Elaine began watching them closely, carefully noting every turn they made as they proceeded deeper into the older sections of the colony. It became easier and easier to keep her cover as they moved into areas with more social activity, even this late at night. She kept a close eye on "Leo"—who was she kidding, it was totally Brad, she caught that much at least when they locked eyes—in particular.

As the group moved into a more lively, populated section of the colony, they all removed their scarves, revealing their faces. Elaine definitely recognized the guy that led the gang earlier, as well as the poor sap whose nose got broken in the scuffle. *No rest for the wicked, I guess*, Elaine caught herself thinking, feeling a bit sorry for the poor guy. Just a bit. He was still involved in gun trafficking, so if anything, she thought he got off lightly. Brad hung back, hesitating to remove his mask, as if he was weighing his options. Elaine could almost see the gears turning, hear the options as they came to Brad. He could slowly disengage from the group, break off, form up with Elaine and Jolene, and then...

something, she wasn't sure what they would do next. He could also stick with the gang, see where they were going, maybe get in and try to find something of note.

As if Brad had read Elaine's mind, he kept pace, still at the back of the group, but still with them. Which is what Elaine would have done had their situations been reversed. Elaine gave a small fist pump, happy to know that they were on the same wavelength.

Rounding another corner, the group entered into what looked to be an old warehouse of some kind, a relic from the founding days of the colony. Elaine began to walk towards the warehouse before she was suddenly stopped by Jolene grabbing her arm. When she looked back in confusion, Jolene whispered, "What exactly is the plan, here?"

"Look, the guy in the back is Brad. I don't know how, exactly, but he knocked another guy out and stole his clothes," Elaine explained.

"Yeah, I gathered that on my own, I'm not stupid," Jolene said, unamused. "I mean...say we follow them all the way back to their hideout, what then?"

"Then...we'll figure it out when we get there! Unless you have any suggestions," Elaine said. "You ask an awful lot of questions, but I don't hear you making any recommendations."

"I just don't want us to end up in a bad situation," Jolene said quietly. "We lucked out last time because the police showed up. We might not be so lucky again, and I'd rather our success, our *survival* be because we did something right, rather than just happening to be in the right place at the right time."

"A lot of the time that's what success *is* though," Elaine argued. "Sure, having a plan and doing the right thing can improve your chances, but just as often a plan going off without a hitch is all down to luck. Sometimes you can do everything right, plan for everything you can think of, and still fail, while some moron just kinda flails his way into victory. It's not fair, but that's just how it is."

"Look, I've seen the *Star Trek* that you're referring to, and I don't disagree, but I don't trust my own luck to not completely screw me when it counts, so I want to do everything in my power to minimize the chances of that happening. Now can we *please* make a plan of some kind?"

Elaine looked at the girl, mouth hanging open. As comparatively quiet as she'd been up to this point, the more forceful air the girl was starting to put on was legitimately surprising to Elaine. She began to stammer out a response, "Right, I'm sorry, any ideas?"

—

Brad wasn't sure what he was expecting when entering into the gangsters' hideout, but he probably should have been less surprised than he was at the ratty old warehouse he found himself in. If he had to guess, it was probably that he hoped their hideout would be somewhat more modern or well-stocked, given their association with an industry as lucrative as gun smuggling. Or at least, as lucrative as Brad had imagined gun smuggling to be, as dangerous as it was. If Brad were a gun runner, no doubt his rates would be able to pay for more than this dinky shack considering the inherent risk, but Brad also might not have to keep at least seven more people under his employ. Probably more, knowing Brad's luck.

Brad cast his eyes around the warehouse, counting at least four other people that weren't with the gang in black. In total that made for eleven possible hostiles if Brad wasn't careful. No way in hell he was taking this mask off now, even though the others had already removed theirs.

Besides that and some papers strewn across the table in this makeshift sitting room/living quarters, nothing jumped out at Brad as particularly suspicious. Well, any more suspicious than a bunch of gang bangers living out of an unused warehouse already was, at any rate.

Brad eyed the messy stack of papers a little more closely. The font was too small to be legible in any sort of detail, but a few words and phrases stuck out at him, such as "Mars", "seven caches", "independence", and "nosy detective", that last one Brad took personally.

This wasn't much to go on, so Brad thought he'd try to push for more information.

"Hey boss," Brad began in his attempted disguised voice, "what exactly are we doing here? Like, for Matsumoto?"

"You hit your head, Leo?" a big guy with bleached hair, a gold tooth, and a pierced eyebrow that Brad could now see more clearly—this guy must have been the boss—asked, raising his pierced eyebrow. "We're hired muscle for his little gun-running shindig. You seemed all for it a while ago."

Brad winced. *Should have thought that question through, but I gotta keep pushing. Deflect!* "Uh, yeah, I guess I was. I dunno, that detective guy did clock me pretty good. Maybe I'm wondering if it's worth it."

"Look, whatever the big guy does with the guns is his own business. I didn't ask any questions when negotiating for pay, and frankly I don't give a rat's ass what he does with them as long as those paychecks keep coming in. I'd advise you to stop worrying about it, capiche?"

"Right. Yes sir," Brad said in a feigned sheepish voice.

"Yes sir?" the big man asked in disbelief. "Man, you really did hit your head." He crossed over to a refrigerator in the corner of their little sitting area, pulling out a can of the cheapest beer that could be found in a local grocery store. Cracking it open and plopping down on a nearby sofa, the man said, "Hey Leo, you can take the mask off now, man. We're safe. Relax."

Brad stiffened. "Uhh, no thanks, I'm not feeling the best. I think I'm just gonna head out. Catch you guys later?"

The big guy leaned in closer, "What, you got some place to be? C'mon, let's hang out and celebrate a completed mission! That detective's out of our hair, and Matsumoto might even give us a bigger cut of the profits. Let's crack one open, man!"

"No, I'm really not feeling that good, boss." Brad began to make his way towards the entrance.

"Ah shit," the guy who stuck up for "Leo", a shorter, dark-skinned man, said excitedly, "Leo's got a date! Let's hear it, did you finally seal the deal with that hot waitress?"

"Uh...yeah, you caught me," Brad stammered. *Oh god what have I gotten myself into now?*

"Hell yeah, brother!" the guy exclaimed. "I knew you two were a good match. I seen the way she looks at you when we hit that bar."

The leader frowned. "Never woulda taken you for a Bro Code violator, Leo, letting some chick come between you and the guys. Gotta say I'm a little disappointed, man."

Brad's hair stood on the back of his neck. "Oh yeah, that's me, total Bro Code violator. Well, don't wait up for me. It's gonna be a long night, if ya feel me." His pace towards the entrance picked up.

"Wait," the leader said. "What was her name, again?" he asked, feigning a casual, interested tone.

Oh come on!

"Uh...her name...uhh...well...it's um..."

"Out with it man, you either know her name or you don't. She only serves us every time we hit that place. Now what's her name?" the leader pushed.

"C'mon boss, don't put him on the spot like that. You know it's been a while since he got dumped by Jin-ju. Lighten up, man," the defender suggested. "He's clearly nervous."

"Yeah!" Brad said, feigning a surge of confidence. "That's right, I'm just nervous, her name is definitely..." *Random name, go!* "Aimee."

The leader looked at Brad blankly. "Aimee...?"

"Yep. Aimee," Brad said firmly.

The two stared at each other for an agonizingly long time.

"Nah man, that's not her name," the defender said.

DAMMIT!

"Oh, now that's interesting," the leader said. "I coulda sworn you knew her name considering how much you talk about how pretty she is. Never woulda taken you for a guy who forgets something so important."

"Oh, it's not that big a deal, he's nervous, of course he got Aimee mixed up with Emmy."

Okay now that's just bull*shit,* Brad thought to himself.

"Uh, right, yeah, sorry, it's that cold. Look, I gotta go or I'm gonna be late."

Frowning, the leader leaned back into the couch. "Whatever man. It better be a good date. We've been waiting for you to make your move for months. You screw this up and you're fired."

"Right, of course," Brad stammered, "Good one. See you guys later!" He awkwardly shuffled out the door.

As Brad walked away from the warehouse, the thought of a possible war for independence turned over in his mind. He had no real attachment to the colony, nor did he want anything to do with a war in general.

When he was a satisfactory distance away from the warehouse, he tore the scarf away from his face, gasping for the freshly recycled colony air that he could now enjoy without some other guy's sweat in his mouth, drawing the attention of two passing police officers.

Oh wait, that's...

"Hey Elaine," Brad stammered. "Let's go now. Please. My office. Please."

Chapter 15

The three of them returned to Brad's office in complete silence. At one point Jolene had opened her mouth to ask a question but Elaine shot her a look that clearly meant, "Not now." Thus, the subject waited.

As they stepped into his office and Brad locked the door, he crossed to his refrigerator, somewhat regretting turning down the drink from the gangsters. He regretted it even more once he opened his fridge and saw that his own supply was depleted. Disappointed, Brad plopped down on his sofa, staring at the ceiling. After a little bit, he finally said, "You guys hungry? I'm starving, and nobody thought to feed me while I was in jail."

Jolene finally mustered up the gumption to ask, "What the hell happened to you?" a question that was met with a glare of disbelief from Elaine that Jolene merely shrugged at.

Brad blinked. "Oh yeah, sorry, I guess I didn't really explain. Sorry. A lot to process, let's go from the top. I got arrested when you guys disappeared. Matsumoto tried to pay me off to drop the case. I said no. He sent in a guy to rough me up a little so

I'd be more receptive to his offer. His guy is currently locked up in my cell, with my favorite jacket and pair of jeans that I'll probably never see again. Also apparently I made that guy look like a Bro Code violator to his buddies for bailing on a night of drinking with the bros for a date."

"Sounds like your average Saturday night," Elaine quipped. "So what's bothering you?"

"Oh, right, the gangsters are just hired muscle to help Matsumoto with his gun smuggling ring. I saw some papers in their hideout that talked about seven caches in total and something about Martian independence, so that's something to look forward to I guess," Brad answered.

"Wait wait wait, Martian independence?" Elaine asked incredulously. "I didn't realize there was any movement of the sort."

"There isn't, as far as I've been able to tell," Brad said. "Probably some pocket of extremists who want to keep "the Man" off their lawn, or whatever. But they've clearly got money for smuggled guns, and a lot of them from the sound of things. Which can't be good."

"I had no idea that Matsumoto was pulling for something like that," Elaine said, folding her arms.

"Oh yeah," Brad suddenly remembered. "The stuff on the hard drive should have hit the net by now. Let's see what people are saying.

Sure enough, a quick search showed that, like a pack of vultures, news organizations from the Epiphany Colony all the way back to Earth had swarmed on the news as it broke, with particularly scathing headlines. Brad opened one article titled "Fact Check: Are the Police Smuggling Guns in Your Neighborhood?" grinning at the absurdity, laughing as he read what was written.

EPIPHANY COLONY—An anonymous source leaked the contents of a hard drive to Earth-based message boards at approximately 9 PM local time with documents allegedly tying local police captain Shoji Matsumoto to a firearm smuggling ring based on the Epiphany Colony, leading to an outcry for his arrest and interrogation as well as an increase of skepticism towards police forces throughout Earth Federation space. The original post can be found here.

At this time nobody has been able to confirm the poster's identity or location. When we reached out to Mr. Matsumoto for comment we received no response at this time.

Mr. Matsumoto, a transplant from Earth, is an alumnus of the University of Luna at Nubium's Criminal Justice program, with a decorated service record in previous assignments throughout Federation space. However, not much is known about the man behind the badge besides his previous marriage to Professor Wei Xieren at the ULN's law school. Professor Wei has declined to comment at this time.

We will continue to update the story as it develops.

Brad's journey through the social media response to the article and the news breaking in general was equal parts entertaining and disturbing. While the occasional nugget of decent, respectful discussion could be found, it really was the proverbial diamond in the rough as people turned to personal attacks and insults as lines were quickly drawn in the sand over those who believed the story versus those who thought the story and stories like it were a concerted assault on an innocent man's character. Throughout the war of words, Brad discovered pockets of responses citing the very incident as a perfect example of why the federation should give way to smaller, more independent states.

The irony was too much for Brad as he leaned back in his chair, laughing. For a brief moment Brad found himself eternally grateful that these people were separated by cyberspace and the mask of anonymity, or else the wars throughout the nets would have been enough to fan the flames of his already-growing fear of a looming war in the real world.

Still, the lack of comment from Matsumoto or the ex-wife that nobody had even realized existed before now was something that made Brad uncomfortable. That could be an angle to examine, if she'd pick up the phone or answer an email. Though he also felt bad for her. Being a professor at one of the Federation's highest ranking law schools would mean that she was already extremely busy, and the sudden influx of reporters wanting her attention because of this erupting political scandal would probably mean she was away from any form of long distance communication for the foreseeable future.

Still, it never hurts to try.

Brad pulled up a blank email to send to Professor Wei, unsure of how to open it.

Dear Prof. Wei,

Brad shook his head. People hadn't opened an email with "Dear So-and-so" since the 2100's.

Good Morning, Professor Wei,

No, that felt weird as well. It wasn't morning where Brad was, and it would look even sillier if she opened the email at any point besides the morning.

Brad rolled his eyes. *Let's just do the bare minimum.*

Professor Wei

I can only imagine how much harassment you're getting from news companies and pranksters, so I'm going to cut directly to the chase. I'm a private detective, and my current case is directly related to the gun smuggling ring. It wasn't at the beginning of the case, but you understand how things can kind of get flipped on their heads as an investigation proceeds, given your own profession.

I suppose I have two big questions.

1. Did you know anything about your ex-husband's possible link to a gun trafficking ring?

2. Did your ex-husband have any affiliation with Martian supremacy or Martian independence movements?

I understand how out-of-left-field that second one is, but there's a reason for it. During my investigation into the gun trafficking ring I discovered some documents linking them to a Martian independence movement. As far as I've been able to tell in my search, any groups claiming to be in support of Martian independence tend to be small but extremely vocal groups of isolationists, but any information I can find will not only help my own investigation, but it will also prove vital to the Federation's own official investigation that's no doubt on the horizon.

I am prepared to take your word at face value, whatever it may be. I understand that following your divorce, you might not want anything to do with whatever your ex-husband has found himself in the middle of, and if it had started while you two were still married, the damage is already done.

Thank you for your time.

Brad Asher
Private Investigator

Brad sent the email off. He'd noticed that he rambled a bit while writing, but he was much too tired to proofread any professional communications at the moment.

He looked up, seeing Elaine and Jolene still in the office. *Oh yeah, I forgot about that.*

"So...how about that dinner?" Brad asked.

Chapter 16

The rest of the evening passed in relative silence as the three of them waited for any response at all from Professor Wei. In the meantime, Elaine had slipped out long enough to get some food from one of the few stores open at this hour. Eventually, the discussion turned to the group's plans for the rest of the investigation.

"So say she actually writes you back," Elaine began. "What exactly are you going to do with the information she gives you? We already have a pretty big case even without his ties to Martian separatists."

"I guess I just want to know why, y'know? He has a good job without the risk of the gun smuggling racket." Brad folded his arms. "I guess it would help if I had half an idea of what Martian separatists even want or why they want to separate themselves from the Federation."

"We can worry about that if we have to later on. There's no sense in borrowing trouble about something that might not even apply," Jolene broke in. "We've got enough to worry about with the case at hand. Let's just focus on the here and now."

As Brad opened his mouth to respond, his communicator buzzed. He quickly dove at his desk to see what the notification was.

One unread message. From Wei Xieren.

"Hey, she actually got back to us!" Brad exclaimed as he opened the message, quickly skimming the contents.

After a few seconds of silence, Jolene cleared her throat, and Elaine said, "Well c'mon man, don't leave us hanging."

"Oh, sorry," Brad responded sheepishly, before beginning to read.

Mr. Asher

You weren't wrong when you said you put me on the spot with your questions, nor were you wrong in assuming that there would be a flood of messages, requests for comment, and pranks. In fact there is a part of me right now that believes this whole thing is a hoax, but your name kind of surprised me so I thought I'd look into you a little bit. You're a detective on the Epiphany Colony, which narrowed the field of search results for one Brad Asher quite a bit, so imagine my surprise when I found out you're the son of Mikhail and Edna Asher. A big name in the field of private security and a doctor, respectively. Quite a pedigree you've got there. Long story short, this feels a little too deliberate and well-detailed to just be a prank or a hoax, so... what the hell, I'll indulge you.

I regret to say that I know nothing about Shoji's links to a gun smuggling ring of any kind. If he had anything to do with it beforehand while we were still together, he hid it quite well, though I find myself doubtful that that is the case. It certainly isn't what caused our divorce, if that's what you were driving at. Though who knows? It's been a few years. Maybe after he was transferred from Luna to the outer colonies, he made some buddies.

And before you ask, yes, he transferred not long after we got divorced. He said it would be easier to not have to see me in a professional sense, which...I hate to admit it, but he was right.

As far as whether or not he has ties to Martian separatists, no, that doesn't feel like him. He's said he's altogether unimpressed with those movements. Or at least, he was. Like anything else, in the years since his transfer, maybe things have changed.

I wish I had more to add, but unfortunately, I really don't. After we split up we haven't had much to do with one another, and from the sound of things with this case and its mounting controversy, that's probably for the best. I'll happily answer any other questions you have, but forgive me if I'm slow to respond or don't have much more for you. Just please, get to the bottom of this before he hurts himself and anyone else.

Sincerely,

Wei Xieren, JD—Professor of Law at University of Luna at Nubium

Brad winced at that last sentence. He could only hope they could put a stop to this before someone else got hurt. The good news was that Brad, Elaine, and Jolene were at the top of Matsumoto's hit list. On the other hand, it wasn't going to stop with them. Though now that his crimes were out in the open, perhaps his hit list had just gotten too long to manage. The stone had begun rolling down the hill. Heaven help anyone who got in its way.

As he mused about this, Jolene piped up, "By the way, has there been any news about Matsumoto? Surely he's responded to these allegations by now."

Elaine frowned. "You don't think he's going to try to brush it off or ignore it? Anyone could fabricate some spreadsheets."

"Sure," Brad said hesitantly, "but that's a lot of detail to fake. Let's see if there's any news."

Brad quickly scanned through the morning newsfeed. While it was only about 3 AM, Brad was almost certain that there would at least be an acknowledgement somewhere. Sure enough, he found one article from the same organization that had put out the clickbait hours before, entitled "Police Captain Speaks Out!"

This oughta be good, Brad thought to himself as he opened the article before sighing in disappointment at its short length.

EPIPHANY COLONY—Following allegations of his involvement in a local gun smuggling ring, Police Captain Shoji Matsumoto has agreed to hold a press conference. Will update the story with details as they arise.

Brad chuckled. Clearly they were pulling double duty at this particular place. He looked at the name of the company, expecting some nonsense title like *Conspiracies Monthly* or *The Tin Foil Herald*. He was disappointed, in fact, to find that the site was called *The Epiphany Daily Standard*, not a particularly unpopular news source, though not considered the most reliable. Brad quickly cross-referenced the information presented in the article, finding others that had announced a press conference for the following morning at 11 AM, but nothing beyond that.

Brad had noticed his eyes were beginning to burn as fatigue washed over him. He had been awake for almost a full day, after all. As Brad looked up from his computer, he noticed that Elaine's eyes were glazed over with the look of someone whose caffeine stores had run out hours ago, while Jolene had leaned into her arm to hide the fact that she was fast asleep. At this point, Brad straightened up and said, "It's late, and we've got a few hours until this press conference. We should get some sleep. It's not much, but we've got the couches out here and there are some blankets in that closet," Brad said, indicating a small wardrobe behind the desk.

"What, you're not going to offer your bed to your guests?" Elaine said dryly.

If he wasn't so tired, Brad might have made a joke about fitting the three of them on his crummy queen-sized mattress, but all he could manage was a simple, "Nope. Maybe next time, Sport. Of course, you're welcome to try your luck at your own places."

Elaine rolled her eyes. "Fine, enjoy your nap, Your Majesty," she said with all the enthusiasm of a fourteen-year-old getting up at 5 AM for band practice.

"You don't have to tell me twice."

—

Brad had half expected to spend a half hour or more tossing and turning, trying to fall asleep. However, he didn't even remember falling asleep once he plopped down on his bed, and if it weren't for the alarm that he'd set, he likely wouldn't have woken up for the press conference. As he staggered out into the main room of his office, he noticed that Elaine and Jolene had already pulled up the conference on the main viewscreen with a small breakfast of various quick snacks they'd purchased from a local convenience store, including some cheap coffee that Brad assumed was fake, but he was too tired to care.

The conference was streamed via the net from Matsumoto's office, shared to all major news sources within Federation Space. The whole thing was remarkably well-organized and profes-sional, including Matsumoto's own appearance: clean-shaven, freshly pressed uniform, and if Brad's own eyes deceived him, there was a small bit of foundation on his face, perhaps to cover up any wrinkles or blemishes. Whatever it was that Matsumoto had to reveal, he certainly was pulling out all the stops for it.

He had already begun speaking, laying out the timeline for the allegations.

"...It is with great regret that I must inform you all that what has been discovered about me is true. I have been using my position within the police force to sponsor a gun smuggling ring for quite some time," he said, in what appeared to be a sincere tone. If it wasn't, Brad was certain it was an award-worthy performance.

"I abused my station for monetary gain, and in doing so I betrayed the trust placed upon me by the general public as well as those officers who view me as their superior," he continued, staring unblinkingly into the camera, likely where his teleprompter was. "Or should I say, 'viewed', as I will now be tendering my resignation, effective immediately. In addition, I will be handing myself over to the authorities..."

This got Brad's attention. For someone who was so certain last night that he was on top of things, he'd surely given up quickly. Suspiciously quickly...

Oh no...

Brad looked at Elaine and Jolene, hoping that he wasn't the only one who found this odd. "How long do you think it'll take us to get to his office?" Brad asked frantically.

Elaine definitely seemed to have picked up on whatever signals Brad was putting out, because she responded, "Too long for us to be able to do anything about whatever's going to happen to him."

Jolene raised an eyebrow. "What do you mean, 'whatever's going to happen to him'?"

Brad quickly responded, "He's in danger, either from his clients or from someone higher up the food chain. Why else wouldn't he try to brush the whole thing aside with what little corroborating evidence there has been?" He quickly stood up. "I gotta at least try to get there."

Without waiting for a response, he quickly dashed out the door.

Chapter 17

As Brad quickly dashed through the thoroughfare towards the police department's headquarters, he noticed quite a bit of foot traffic in the section of the colony that housed the headquarters building. Perhaps they were hoping to catch a glimpse of the procession as Matsumoto was hauled off. Surely nothing would happen with this many people around, right?

Although it wasn't as if Brad had a specific plan in mind for when he arrived at the station or procession or wherever he currently found him dashing off to. He'd just hoped that, because he connected *some* dots, he might be able to see something going wrong before it happened. As he passed by a restaurant, he could hear fragments of Matsumoto's press conference as well as the livid reactions of the people within. Just judging from the tones of the voices he heard as he dashed through this section of the colony, Brad was almost certain a riot would form if left unchecked.

No time for that right now! Brad thought to himself. *We can't let Matsumoto get away, but we also can't let anyone silence him since he's the key to this whole thing!*

As he drew closer to the station, Brad noticed a remarkably large number of people in green maintenance jumpsuits throughout the area, each wearing a low baseball cap. *Okay, surely someone else realizes how suspicious this looks, right?*

Almost as if they were waiting for something. Though Brad couldn't just assume they were the only ones that would try to pull something. Perhaps they had some others dressed as security or in other outfits. Really, anyone here could be dangerous, so best not to make any assumptions until they got to work. Whatever that work was.

Brad quickly pulled his communicator out and fired off a message to Elaine.

There are a bunch of suspicious-looking guys near the station.

A reply came not long after.

Yeah, we noticed. You left us so fast we had to lock the door behind you. We're almost there.

Brad grimaced. That definitely didn't look good for him. Too late to worry about that though.

He looked towards the front entrance to the police headquarters as a crowd congregated around the doors, all shouting angrily. Brad chuckled, imagining the group carrying things like torches and pitchforks before shaking himself out of that fantasy. Right.

Someone's life was still at risk here.

The doors slid open as a group of officers wearing Federation military riot gear strode out, shoving and shouting for the mob to make way as Matsumoto was led out, his hands behind his back in handcuffs. Brad watched as a man threw a cup full of *something* at the cuffed officer before he was tackled to the ground, shouting a stream of curses as he was restrained and hauled off. Surprisingly, this didn't satiate the crowd's lust for violence and vengeance as they began pushing against the entourage of riot officers. Brad caught himself feeling kind of bad for the officers. The only bad thing they had done was report to work that morning and they were catching hell over something someone else did.

Brad shook his head, bringing himself back to reality. *Can't make any assumptions. We don't know who is on which side out here.*

Almost as an answer to Brad's line of thinking, the air around him exploded, as the sound of a gunshot echoed throughout the domed walls of the colony. Immediately, Brad's ears rang, drowning out any and all sound around him as he saw the crowd scatter. Brad quickly looked at the throng of officers escorting Matsumoto, or at least where Matsumoto *was*.

Some blood had splattered against an officer, and though he couldn't make out their voices, Brad could tell one was ordering the others to fan out and find the one responsible while they saw to Matsumoto's wound. At least, that's who Brad assumed was wounded.

Brad cursed, looking around the immediate vicinity but finding no leads. He looked back at the now smaller squad of officers, raising an eyebrow at what he saw.

They'd already slid Matsumoto's body onto a stretcher and covered it with a tarp. *Seems a little early to pronounce the man dead,* Brad caught himself thinking before ducking behind a corner, trying to keep out of sight. If he hadn't already been spotted, at any rate.

The men surrounding the stretcher worked quickly, leaving a remarkably similar-looking mannequin to Matsumoto at the scene of the shooting as they quickly wheeled the real one around the side of the building into a small vehicle that looked like a repurposed XL golf cart with the back rows of seats removed to create a miniature pickup truck. It happened so quickly Brad almost wondered if he imagined the whole thing happening. But no, they definitely just took off with the captain under a tarp, and from the looks of things, the little cart wasn't headed towards the hospital.

Rather, it seemed to be heading towards the space docks. Brad quickly placed a call to the police. Once the receptionist answered, Brad quickly said, "Look, I just saw some people take off with Captain Matsumoto and I don't have much time to explain. Something's about to happen at the docks. A bomb, a kidnapping, a hijacking, something, I don't know, all I'm saying is get every officer you can spare down there."

The receptionist paused before saying, "Are you calling in a bomb threat?"

Oh for—wait a minute...

"Uh...yes, yes I am."

—

As Elaine and Jolene rushed to catch up with Brad, they heard the deafening pop of a gunshot in the distance. Elaine slowed to a halt, before shouting, "Shit, we're too late!"

Now that they'd stopped, Jolene asked, "Okay what's going on?"

"Someone killed Matsumoto," Elaine began. "They got him out of the way so that he couldn't blab about the locations of the gun caches." Sure enough, as though in response to the gunshot, a huge stampede of people began pouring out from the direction of police HQ. However, Elaine thought she could see a small handful of people making their way through the crowd *toward* HQ's square, wearing an assortment of outfits ranging from maintenance uniforms to paramedic uniforms to even casual clothing. The paramedics she could believe, but the others were what set off her sketchy-senses.

She began to slowly tail the small group of people before her communicator suddenly went off, signaling an emergency transmission from HQ. She looked at the screen, anticipating a call, but saw it was sent out first as a text message.

Bomb threat at the space docks. Caller hasn't asked for a ransom. All available units are to report to the docks immediately to investigate and attempt to contain the incident.

Elaine glowered. She knew she was onto something, but she wasn't sure how she could justify abandoning her post, because she was *technically* available...

...however, she also had someone in protective custody and it wouldn't do well to put her in such obvious danger. She turned to Jolene and shook her head, noticing that the girl had obviously received the same message. She nodded towards the group of suspicious individuals pushing against the crowd and started walking, making an effort to follow them. As they tailed the group, they noticed that, rather than breaking off at police HQ, they started heading in the direction of the old warehouse that Brad had ended up in the night before. Outside the warehouse was a small motorized cart that was being stocked with duffel bags full of what Elaine could only assume were guns.

Ahh, they're packing up their stuff and trying to leave in the confusion. The bombing at the docks must just be a diversion.

She quickly radioed into HQ.

"Seol here. Sorry for the radio silence the last couple days. I've been looking into this whole gun smuggling thing off the books. Anyway, I think I found one of their caches." She quickly rattled off the coordinates of the warehouse. "Please be advised the suspects are likely armed and dangerous. I know we're already diverting whatever backup we have to the docks, but we're gonna need some backup my way as well."

The response came back quickly. "Acknowledged. Unfortunately we're stretched pretty damn thin. We've gotta prioritize the docks."

"They're leaving their location!" Elaine broke in.

"Try to stall them if you can," the dispatcher said apologetically. "We'll get you someone down there when we can spare them."

Elaine cursed. Her best option was shooting out the tires, but if she did that, especially around here where there wasn't as much of a place to hide, she was screwed. But she *couldn't* let them get away. She quickly glanced sideways at Jolene, saying, "Go find a place to hide. I'm about to kick the hornet's nest."

Chapter 18

As the vehicle was being loaded, Elaine watched for an opening to slip in to mess up the tires. All told there were four people, all from the night before, trying to pack things up, though Elaine was almost certain there were more inside. Sneaking close enough to knife the tires would be difficult. She needed a distraction of some kind.

She watched a little more closely. The group had all returned inside following a request from one of them for extra help lifting something heavy. All except the driver, who sat in his seat, bored, tired eyes on his communicator. Based on the estimate that Elaine could make by seeing him seated like that, he probably stood at least a head, possibly head and shoulders over Elaine's petite frame, but Elaine thought that if she could catch him off-guard, she could at least shove him out of the driver's seat. She slid closer to the vehicle, hiding by the side out of sight, before swinging through the open passenger side, kicking him square in the face.

As he cried out in surprise and threw his arms up, she braced herself against the metal bar she had used to swing in, and, using both her legs as leverage, gave him a good shove out the side of the vehicle.

Now's my chance! Elaine slipped into the driver's seat, gleefully noting that the keys were still in the ignition and the engine was turned on, clearly intended for a quick getaway once the vehicle was fully loaded. Well, whatever the last bag or crate or whatever was, it was all they were being left with as Elaine slammed her foot on the gas pedal, shooting off into the distance as the driver lay there screaming and confused.

That is before she heard a few gunshots pop off after her, bullets colliding with the side of the vehicle before she rounded a corner away from the warehouse.

—

Jolene heard the gunshots coming from the direction of the warehouse before she saw the the cart laden down by the duffel bags come screaming around the corner, Elaine in the driver's seat with a creepy, almost bloodthirsty grin on her face, like this was something she'd waited her whole life to do. It was the most she'd emoted since Jolene had met her, which was probably the most off-putting part, but Jolene couldn't help but find the excitement infectious. If only she had any idea where Elaine was going.

From what Jolene could remember of the map of the colony and the places she'd been in her short time here, it looked like she was heading full speed towards...the spacedock? Jolene quickly sprinted after the cart, knowing full well she had no chance of catching up to it. By now the spacedock would be swarming with other officers, whereas the people ransacking the warehouse—or *warehouses*—likely wouldn't be far behind.

—

Brad cursed his own impulsiveness. *Calling in a bomb threat. What was I thinking? Now I'm going to have to ditch this communicator or at least serve some time behind bars, though hopefully I can spin it as an anonymous tip.*

As he continued running in the direction of the docks, keeping *just enough* distance from the cart that carried Matsumoto's body, likely still alive. The cart wasn't making any detours. They were headed for the docks come hell or high water. As he continued his run, a thought occurred to Brad. A high-ranking government official was just shot in public. The docks were going to be completely locked down for searches. How were they planning on getting around that?

The cart suddenly made a left turn, breaking the path to the docks. *Crap, did they see me?*

Brad quickly mapped out that direction in his mind. They couldn't be looking for any side streets or places to hide. The most notable thing in that direction was an airlock for disposal of non-biodegradable and non-compostable waste. The kind of things that would be shipped off to a processing or disposal plant off-colony.

Brad looked on in disbelief, also annoyed that this hadn't

occurred to him.

They're sneaking him out in a garbage skiff. Those crafty bastards!

The only hole in that plan was the fact that the garbage dock would open to hard vacuum, which seemed counterproductive to sneaking a criminal off-colony. Unless...

Brad noticed himself getting distracted and shook himself back to reality. As he sprinted after the cart, he quickly placed a call to Elaine.

"Can't this wait? I'm kinda busy!" Elaine replied frantically, skipping any pleasantries.

"They're sending him out with the trash!"

"They're spacing him?" Elaine responded in a confused tone. "Look, I really can't talk right now, I—oh dammit—" Brad heard a crash followed by a quick, "SORRY MR. VALENTINE! Look, I just destroyed another cart full of...well something, I've got some goons on my ass and they're really, *really* mad because I stole their ride and most of their stuff, I gotta go!" The line went dead.

At least Brad had an idea of where they were going. Maybe his guardian angel or whoever was tracking his communicator would have backup waiting for him at the garbage dock.

—

"I hope your department's insurance policy can cover this!" Ziggy Valentine's enraged voice carried after Elaine as she quickly sped past the smashed pile of crates, grateful to whatever god was watching over her that somehow her cart had been undamaged, though she was certain that it felt somewhat lighter. She quickly cast her eyes into the bed of the cart before her attention snapped back to the crowded streets in front of her.

Yep, I think I lost a bag there. Hopefully Mr. Valentine just turns it over to the police because I can't go back for it. Maybe Jolene can recover it.

Except now what do I do?

Brad's tipoff about the garbage dock was something she definitely couldn't let slide, but if she hadn't fully escaped her pursuers, breaking off to head the gangsters off at the garbage dock was a bad idea. She couldn't give away every card in her hand like that.

She quickly checked the mirror for any sign of the pursuers. She'd made quite a bit of distance and the shouting and gunfire had ceased a while back, but she couldn't be too sure. She quickly scanned the scenery behind her, noticing nothing except the smashed crates that she'd just passed.

Ah hell, I'll do it.

She quickly changed course for the garbage docks. Eyes forward, she actually noticed someone sprinting along the path. As she squinted, she realized it was Brad, hopelessly trying to catch another cart that she could barely make out in the distance. She slowed down just enough that her quick suggestion of, "BRAD! JUMP ON!" didn't sound *completely* insane.

Brad, startled at the sudden noise, looked back, and for a brief instant Elaine could see him making the calculations before swinging into the passenger seat using the same bar she had just a few minutes ago to steal the cart.

"Just you?" Brad asked, desperately trying to catch his breath. Elaine felt for the guy. He clearly wasn't doing enough cardio.

"Just me," Elaine responded flatly.

"What are you going to do?" Brad asked.

"Something really stupid."

Suddenly, sirens split the air as Elaine noticed a few police vehicles come screaming up behind them.

"Oh yeah, I'm the one who made the bomb threat. So I'm not surprised they were able to zero in on me," Brad explained through gasps for air.

Fantastic.

The airlock for the trash dock quickly appeared in their view, growing steadily closer. Brad and Elaine could see a cart near the door as someone stepped out to open it.

"That's them! You should start slowing down!" Brad said.

Elaine ignored him.

"Aren't you going to slow down?" Brad asked, a tinge of fear in his voice.

Elaine continued ignoring him, setting a course directly for the cart.

"Elaine?"

"Brad, you might wanna brace yourself," Elaine said flatly as she rammed the other cart at full speed. Time seemed to slow to a crawl as their cart smashed through the other cart, sending its passengers and contents as well as the contents directly behind Elaine flying into the air. Brad and Elaine kept a white-knuckle grip on whatever they could inside their cart to avoid being ejected as time slowed to a crawl. It seemed their forward momentum would never end as the man at the door controls screamed, diving to the side.

Although she was sure she hadn't been hit by anything, every-thing hurt. Brad's complexion had gone a few shades whiter than he already was as he muttered, "Elaine...let's not do that again. Ever."

The other police vehicles screeched to a halt as officers poured out of them, weapons drawn.

Epilogue

EPIPHANY COLONY—*Thursday morning following the now confirmed staged shooting of police captain Shoji Matsumoto, a small group of organized criminals with alleged ties to Martian separatists were detained attempting to flee the colony with millions of credits' worth of untagged firearms and ammunition via spacedock. Connections to a previously thought to be unrelated accident at the trash dock have since been confirmed, as members of this group had attempted to smuggle the body of Shoji Matsumoto out of the colony via a paid-off trash skiff bound for Mars.*

The police captain had not only survived the shooting, but was completely unharmed, instead rupturing a blood bag at the time of the shooting, and the gun behind the shooting was confirmed through police investigation to have been loaded with blanks. The purpose behind the shooting was to fake the captain's death for reasons that can only be speculated upon at this time.

Among those injured in the accident were local police officer Elaine Seol and private detective Brad Asher. Both were detained for questioning following being examined by medical officials, and both have been released at this time.

As the story continues to develop, updates will be provided.

Related, local grocer Ziggy Valentine is pursuing damages following a wrongful arrest due to suspected ties to the group following discovery of a duffel bag full of firearms within a destroyed shipment intended for his store...

Brad couldn't help but laugh at the last bit when Jolene, in an embarrassed panic, showed him the clipped news article. While she hadn't been named as the officer who detained Mr. Valentine, the fact that it was a mistake she'd made clearly embarrassed her greatly.

"Don't laugh!" she exclaimed. "I ought to sue that quack journalist for defamation here! Everyone saw it, everyone knows it was me!"

Elaine took a sip of her coffee and then said, "Relax, it's not as if you're the only one who accidentally arrested an innocent man in the heat of the moment, and I would have probably done the same, to be honest. That guy has always kinda rubbed me the wrong way."

"You're one to talk," Jolene said in a huff. "If the bag hadn't fallen off the cart as you smashed through the shipment I wouldn't have even seen the damn thing!"

"Yeah, and I wouldn't have gotten distracted and run into his crates if *someone* hadn't tried calling me while I was driving!"

Elaine said, glaring at Brad.

"Like I was supposed to know you'd hijacked a cart from a bunch of gangsters!" Brad shot back defensively. "Look, who cares, it's all over. The bad guys are behind bars. All the weapons caches have been found. And there's currently a huge investigation going on down on Mars to find out just how deep this supposed 'insurrection' goes. I call that a win!"

"They missed one," Elaine said dryly.

"What?"

"I said they missed one. They're not reporting it to lessen any potential public panic, but there's still one cache somewhere."

"But I thought Matsumoto said he knew every corner of this colony like the back of his hand," Brad said doubtfully. "How the hell could they miss one?"

"Beats me," Elaine said, taking another sip of her coffee. "Besides, it's not my problem anymore. That was the last straw."

"Yeah, about that," Brad said, "Just what are your plans now?"

"I guess I can't keep surfing by on my savings," Elaine said. "You know anyone who's hiring?"

"Well, no, but..."

"Want some help?"

"I don't think I can afford your rates," Brad said sheepishly.

"Well, look at it this way. You've been ignoring a lot of messages. You clearly could use another hand or two. Plus with my expertise we'll be able to expand past the walls of this colony. Y'know, take the old-fashioned bounty hunter route."

"Yeah, and just where do you plan on getting a ship?" Brad asked, a tinge of annoyance in his tone.

"One step at a time, Brad," Elaine said, relaxing back into the couch.

"Right...and what about you Jolene?"

"Still suspended. Still under investigation and psyche evaluation. They found traces of some drug used in mind control experiments in my blood, so they think that's why Matsumoto was able to get me to try to shoot Elaine."

"Mind control?"

"Yep. Mind control."

"Is this something we're going to need to worry about?" Brad asked, raising an eyebrow.

"That's up to you. Either way, I've got nothing else going on, so...uh...want someone to help you with your paperwork?"

"Yeah, sure, I guess. Though we're going to have to discuss pay later. As soon as I can figure out where the money's coming in in the first place. Either way, I want another week of 'vacation', and then we can get back to it. Deal?"

"Deal," Elaine and Jolene said simultaneously.

About the Author

Aaron Cahoon was born in Burley, Idaho on October 5, 1991. Since there wasn't a wealth of things to do in his hometown, Aaron found himself drawn to the world of fiction through books, movies, tv shows, video games, et cetera, with a special love for sci-fi and fantasy stories when he was able to escape from expectations like sports.

He graduated from Brigham Young University Idaho with a degree in International Studies after serving a two year mission for the Church of Jesus Christ of Latter-Day Saints in South Korea, and his time spent abroad as well as his time spent in his studies have done much to color his perception of the world around him.

Now he lives in Oregon with his wife Karin and their cat Julius.

You can connect with me on:
🌐 https://www.aaroncahoon.net
🐦 https://twitter.com/acahoon2
📘 https://www.facebook.com/aaroncahoonauthor